MW01505219

Praise for *Steppe*

"A family history, a road trip through contemporary Russia, *Steppe* is as unflinching and capacious as the landscape from which it takes its name. Vasyakina is a rare truthsayer, a voice of her generation. I loved this."
—Jessi Jezewska Stevens, author of *Ghost Pains*

"In Vasyakina's prose, grief and isolation become luminous. When reading this dissociative and brilliant novel, one is reminded that to have a father is to inherit a fractured nation."
—Zain Khalid, author of *Brother Alive*

"A gorgeously recursive book about daughters and fathers, about the unknowability, pain, and occasional tragedy of being fathered in the early twenty-first century, and the way we come to understand our own childhoods only as adults, when it's all too late. I don't think I've ever read anything quite like *Steppe*, and at times when I was reading it felt so real and heartbreaking I could hardly stand it."
—Madeleine Watts, author of *Elegy, Southwest*

Praise for *Wound*

"Both an elegy to the dead and a homecoming . . . Raw, hypnotic."
—Fernanda Eberstadt, *The New York Times Book Review*

"Only an author of great skill could hold such disparate material together while also questioning her own method throughout the process . . . Vasyakina successfully folds the untidy past into the unsettled present, demonstrating how inseparable they are to the person she is." —*The Irish Times*

"[An] affecting debut novel." —*The New Yorker*

"Bruisingly honest reflections on gender and trauma, brilliantly mediated by Elina Alter's translation."
—*The Times Literary Supplement*

"An auto-fictional exploration of processing grief through language, and also a meditation on the Russian lesbian lyric—a polyphonic conversation with feminist thinkers across time and space." —*Asymptote*

"Ambitious in scope . . . Vasyakina powerfully encompasses the absurd and expansive universe of what Gogol described as the 'unbridled incomprehensible Rus,' the land with its terrors, its poetry and loftiness and its magic, to the skin and bones of the tender and violent people who inhabit it." —*The Rumpus*

Steppe

Steppe

A NOVEL

Oksana Vasyakina

Translated from the Russian by Elina Alter

CATAPULT   NEW YORK

STEPPE

Copyright © 2026 by Oksana Vasyakina
Translation copyright © 2026 by Elina Alter

First Catapult edition: 2026

ISBN: 978-1-64622-307-7

Library of Congress Control Number: 2025944455

Jacket design by Nicole Caputo
Jacket art: saltwort engraving © Florilegius / Bridgeman Images
Book design by Laura Berry

Catapult
New York, NY
books.catapult.co

Printed in the United States of America

10 9 8 7 6 5 4 3 2 1

Binding itself to the muzzles of Turkish cannons,
the steppe shakes free of shackles,
hefts its mounds and collapses them,
in darkness uproots the tongue
and tugs tighter the loop
on which the truck drags along.

—ALEXEI PARSHCHIKOV,

"The Steppe"

The seeming silence of the steppe is its voice.

—VERA KHLEBNIKOVA

Torso.—Only he who can view his own past
as an abortion sprung from compulsion and need
can use it to full advantage in the present. For what
one has lived is at best comparable to a beautiful
statue which has had all its limbs knocked off in
transit, and now yields nothing but the precious
block out of which the image of one's future must
be hewn.

—WALTER BENJAMIN, "One-Way Street,"

tr. Edmund Jephcott and Kingsley Shorter

Steppe

I've seen the steppe from the window of an airplane. Do you know what it looks like? The steppe looks like a sinewy piece of yellow meat. Dark-orange lines, like heavy serpents, stripe the sands, gray rivers stripe the sands. The steppe is no desert, you can see the life in it. Gray and blue grasses. Chirring insects, cool eels, darting dice snakes in the Volga delta.

I used to think that the steppe resembled a soft belly. Through the window of my father's truck I could see its spread, rolling upward in tiny hillocks. The steppe is sand pierced by grasses and little pale flowers. Never pull off the paved road, my father used to say. Just try veering right or left, get your wheels stuck, and that's the end of you. When you're driving freight, it's best not to make any unnecessary moves anyway, particularly if you're loaded with steel pipe—you're heavy then, you put on speed quickly, and when you slow down, you roll on for a while out of inertia and you can't stop.

He was driving to Volgograd like that once, loaded with pipe, just before dawn. Morning in the steppe is blinding, pink. The entire expanse floods with light, because there's nothing to block it in the steppe. Worn out by his night on the road, my father began drifting off. The truck rolled down the level highway, and sleep spread over him like a large warm palm. Spread over him and shoved him forward, and he was woken by a screech and a howl. The truck was still moving, but slowly. He looked in the rearview mirror: in the road behind him lay a large metal pancake, blue-white in color. Two drunk traffic cops, going two hundred kilometers an hour after a night out, had driven into the oncoming lane. Traveling toward the cops on the empty morning road was a MAZ truck loaded with pipe, my father asleep at the wheel. The speedy little Mercedes slipped beneath the truck, nudging it lightly in the belly, and contracted, crushing within itself two male bodies slack with drink and sleep.

My father faced no consequences, because it was obvious that only a Mercedes could have managed that maneuver. He was nearly deaf by then, and the metallic screech he'd heard in his sleep hardly disturbed him. So now I got back at them for everybody, my father said simply. The demise of two traffic cops beneath his truck seemed like justice to him. He didn't feel any guilt, and he wasn't guilty, really: even if he had braked, inertia would've kept him moving forward for some time, and there was no place for him to turn. Some other cops drove out to the scene and threw up their hands—it was an accident. They checked his documents and his packing slip for the pipe. With some regret, they noted that if my father had driven by half an hour later, he wouldn't have met these cops on the road. The Mercedes went under his truck just a few kilometers short of the turn-off for the village where the cops were heading to sleep it off. My father hemmed, thinking that it was their bad luck, because he hadn't slept at all that night, and also because they were bastards.

When you're transporting chickens, you drive to the sound of ceaseless clucking. The birds get loaded underneath the tarp like that, squat cages stacked one on top of the other. On the road, they start to die and rot in the heat. When they unload the bottom layer of cages, it's full of little limp orange-and-white carcasses, all dead or about to be, and the floor of the trailer beneath them is covered in dark, stinking stains and gray-white droppings. It's a mess after driving watermelon, too, because bouncing over bumps, the watermelons crack and leak. Then they spoil and stink. After cargo like that, you have to take a broom and meticulously sweep out the wet wood-plank floor, then blast away, with a high-pressure stream, the ingrained stains of droppings, blood, and fibrous fruit flesh. My father preferred driving pipe. He said that pipe doesn't croak and doesn't spoil. You just load it and go, or you stop and don't bother watching it, no one's going to steal pipe from you, it's too heavy. There was a time when his truck got stolen together with the pipe, but I'll tell you about that later.

Once, the steppe was a garden. People built irrigation systems and grew whatever their hearts desired there; the steppe gets a lot of sunlight, so they could bring in three harvests in a single summer. Meaty, crimson oxheart tomatoes, orange pumpkins, cucumbers, wheat. They used to have all that in the steppe. When you look at it now, it seems to be pure salt marsh wasteland, dotted with blue cloudlets of camel thorns. But that's an illusion: if you give the steppe water, it can do a lot.

Then the people left. Well, not quite left. They stopped working the land. The times had changed. The communal farms blew apart like layers of onion skin. But the pipes from the old irrigation systems remained. They became no one's. They remained simply as objects, buried in the sand and the steppe grasses.

You're wondering how people got hold of the pipe. They just did, they stole it. The land now belonged to no one, and nothing grew there, only the buried pipes rusting away. So, say some small-time businessmen hire a truck through a dispatcher, the truck drives up to a field, and there, along the perimeter, a forklift crane pulls the pipe up from the sand. It gets loaded onto the truck and sent to Moscow, to be sold via Moscow to Astrakhan. My father once drove a load like that to a depot in Moscow, near the Kashira Highway. He stayed there for a few days, waiting to be told where to transfer the load. They called him one morning and said to drive it back where it came from, to Volgograd. Printed out some new paperwork, added a markup to the invoice, and sent him back to the same place they'd dug up the pipe. That's how, from nothing and ceaseless motion, money gets made. I asked my father once if he wasn't bothered by the meaningless of it, driving the pipe to Moscow just to take it back again. He said no, it didn't bother him, so long as he got paid.

Once Raisa, the dispatcher, called my father to tell him about an upcoming pipe shipment. We drove out to a spot by Kapustin Yar and parked in the middle of the steppe. But our contacts didn't show up the next day, or the day after that. They called and promised they would be there in two days: something was the matter with their machinery, either it had broken down or they hadn't stolen it yet. So we drove to the nearest market and picked up vodka, a carton of cigarettes, a few cans of condensed milk, canned stewed meat, two loaves of rye bread, and a little beer. I drank the beer on the way back from the market, while it was still cold.

I asked my father right away how long we would wait. He didn't know how long we would wait. No one knew how long we would wait. It was all up to chance, and this made time grow enormous, unmanageable, and also totally unnecessary. Waiting became more interesting. I ate the entire crust of one loaf, dunking it in condensed milk. Then I cooked pasta on a camper stove. The steppe is wide open, and it's as though you are always naked in it. The gray truck stood in a field wild with wormwood and camel thorn, and we lived in that truck for five days, until they brought us a crane to load the pipe.

Waiting in this world, the world of sprawling gray space, meant rushing things, forcing your will upon them. *Waiting* was something forbidden. We simply had to live. Live through every moment, each meal and bodily function. Calmly, thoroughly chew a mouthful of simple food, smoke a Winston Blue crackling with moisture it had absorbed overnight. Everything had to be done with taste. Life's short, my father said, you come flying from a cunt and you're headed for the grave already.

———

On the very first day, I hopped out of the cabin and began walking away from the road toward the horizon. I walked, hoping the truck would fade from sight, but it was always there behind my back; I walked and walked, but the truck failed to disappear, and eventually I'd had enough and just squatted, pulling down my pants. The stream of urine rolled between my sandals, sweeping along tiny shards of dried grasses and mealy white dust.

In the evenings the steppe sky is delicate, sometimes blue, occasionally pink, like a tongue. In this lucent sky, long white clouds unfurl like rolls of canvas. There is no wind, and everything grows still. Time does not pass. Clouds hover over the earth. Night comes slowly, and only the darkness indicates that something can change here, in the steppe.

As I walked back, the truck loomed larger and larger. Later I stopped going into the steppe and just squatted behind a wheel, in a spot my father couldn't see, and peed there.

In the steppe everything dies of boredom. We ate overcooked white seashell pasta and drank vodka. It was hot, and in the heat I didn't get drunk but turned silent and slow. My father was also sullen from the vodka, and after grumbling some would fall asleep on his grungy sleeper berth.

In daytime, the rumbling of the steppe is subsumed by bright, relentless light. Looking out at that vastness, there is nothing to feel but awe. Awe because the steppe is endless and keeps coming and coming at your eyes. And there's no place in the steppe to hide from it, in the day; it must be endured, acknowledged, and accepted the way it is—great, and a little desolate and monotonous.

Night in the steppe is deafening. It's pitch black, and the chirring in it pierces your body with a thousand needles. It's hard to sleep; the entire steppe seems to be launching itself in your direction. The nighttime steppe is an army of archers aiming their electric black arrows directly at you.

Meanwhile the grasses keep whispering, whispering about some mortal danger, the crickets shriek, and the heat renders your body all too present to itself. It feels like your heart is breaking to pieces there in the nighttime steppe, with the heady fumes of cooling wormwood and hemlock mingling with the scent of your sweat and other salty secretions. In the night-time steppe you come to know your own body resting on thin, threadbare sheets. This gives you a terrible, crushing headache. Wind brings the smells of fire and shit. The steppe bombards you, and in the cabin of the truck you lie as though naked, looking through the dark window.

The insects in the steppe go on chirring, but you can't see them. Birds in the steppe fly by, frolicking, and disappear somewhere in the sky, in distant silence. There's nothing in the steppe to catch your eye; there is only distance. Sometimes the wind brings over a sliver of a plastic cup, you pick it up, and it disintegrates in your hand like ancient parchment. In the steppe everything crumbles and decays. My father tossed his cigarette butts and lemonade bottles right out the window, and when I asked him why he did that, he said that the steppe would take them. The steppe took everything, and it was unclear where all of it went. Everything there fell apart and perished, as though the steppe were a field of deadly frequency, annihilating, on a molecular level, any object that happened into it.

My father loved the steppe, probably because it was a wholly forbearing space. The steppe went on and on, and any danger in it could be spotted from afar. There were vipers and little rat snakes, but they were afraid of loud noises and never showed themselves. Sometimes a tumbleweed rolled through. In the wind its movements could look somewhat animated, so that the tumbleweed appeared to be a breathing body. But it was a dead thing, though it sowed dry, white seeds as it went.

You know, my father had nothing but the steppe, which he thought of as his home. He loved it for its vastness. He had nothing of his own. Even the truck's parking spot in the garage wasn't his; he just used it, it belonged to someone else. In order to park there, he had to pick up his scratched little Samsung and send off a few texts. He didn't know how to make spaces between words in text messages, just as he didn't know how to alternate between lowercase and capital letters, so all his texts were lowercase and punctuated by periods. Like a bike chain. If no one responded to him, he'd call to ask whether a spot at the truck stop was available. They never turned him away, and he'd drive the MAZ over to the stop to clean the cabin and make repairs. There was always something that needed fixing, you can take my word for it.

The truck didn't belong to him, either. He borrowed it from someone to make a few trips and earn some money. To buy a truck of his own he'd have needed a lot of money, but he never saved anything. He loved the spaciousness of the steppe because it cost nothing just to have it and look at it forever. All that space was just there, and my father genuinely did not understand why the rest of the world was so stingy with him.

There were rumors that the Plato system would soon be installed, and then drivers would have to pay not only the truck dispatcher but also the government. Pay them for what, my father wanted to know. They say they'll use the money to fix the roads, they're saying that the loads we drive are ruining them. But what are roads for? he asked. Roads are there so you can drive on them. And the road, whose is it, it's the country's, meaning it belongs to the common man, the driver and the long-distance trucker. I pay Raisa, and I'm a member of the long-distance truckers' bureau, I pay taxes there. So why should I also pay for the roads? When we get to Volgograd Oblast—he said to me as we drove—you'll see what kind of roads they have there. I call Volgograd Dumbograd, because the cops there are dumbasses and they don't fix the roads right, just wham bam and they're done. And what happens if I drive on their wham-bam repair job on Brother here? That's it for their repairs. Because things have to be done thoughtfully, so they last. Not the way those dumbasses do it. Brother was what my father called his truck. Driving into Volgograd Oblast, he began cursing loudly. I could feel the difference with my own ass: the road was so bad that we pulled over every seventy kilometers or so to take a break from the jostling. The rough ride made eating unappealing, and smoking during a drive like that was disgusting, but we still chain-smoked cigarette after cigarette. Not for pleasure, but out of boredom, and our powerlessness before the Volgograd highway.

The men at the garage were saying that the long-distance trucking reforms would do more than oblige my father to pay a ruble and a half per kilometer. The reforms would also introduce a system to track truckers' resting and working hours. A device would be installed to surveil my father: how much time he spent driving, how much time resting. In case of overwork, the system would automatically fine him. But I'm a private contractor, my father said. I don't have time to rest, I don't get a salary like the Magnit guys. Those guys drive around in their German MAN trucks, they sleep when they're supposed to, eat and shit when they're supposed to. They have cameras in their cabins. They're like rabbits, they do everything on schedule. And they take their time, I'll tell you that. They can sleep and still get paid. But I can't sleep, he said. An hour of sleep for me is pretty expensive. If I sleep less and drive more, I'll get the cargo there faster and head back sooner. I can call Raisa, ask what else they've got. Why should I, a free man, drive when they tell me to drive and stay when they tell me to stay?

He wasn't greedy, he never held back from spending money on anything. He just didn't know how to handle it, money. He paid someone fifteen or twenty thousand rubles once a month for the truck and spent just as much on repairs and cleaning. He didn't even have any documents for that truck, just like he didn't have any for his Lada Nine. He simply borrowed a car from someone he knew and once a month let that guy drive the car and paid him some money for it.

Once, driving home after three consecutive trips, he put his entire earnings under the passenger seat cover and lowered both windows. It was the height of spring. Do you know how the steppe blooms in spring? You inhale all that wormwood and you're done for, you're breathing in the steppe. And then those pink shrubs with their little flowers, blossoming like islands of pink mist. Inhale their scent and it's not freedom you're breathing in but sorrow. A sorrowful solitude. My father had rolled down the windows in the cabin to breathe in the steppe, feel that solitude. He turned on his cassette player—he never did get a CD player—and found a tape in the glove compartment, *Mikhail Krug's Golden Hits*. He played the tape and drove on his own way. Drove and sang. Or rather not sang but yelped along happily. And then, out of the corner of his eye, he saw rust-colored birds fluttering from his window. It was the steppe stealing his wages from beneath the passenger seat. Where was he going to look for those five-thousand-ruble bills? The steppe had taken them for itself.

2

I told you that from the window of a plane the steppe resembles a soft stomach. In reality it's hard, beige sand, compressed by the wind. There's density to it. Look at it through the window—it seems welcoming; you ask it to hide you behind a hillock in its white grass, and it beckons you on with the folds of its belly. You walk for a long time toward that little hill, until finally it turns out to be flat and hard, no place to hide behind.

The plastic ribbon of a cassette tape, caught in the sharp, tough grass, whistles in the wind. The tape's turned blue, bleached by the sun, and in the blowing wind, the grass nods along. Nods forlornly, as if it were a person. Everything here is on the move, traveling somewhere. Wind speeds the clouds, wind drags the fragment of a plastic bottle. Somebody used this piece of it as a ladle. It drags and drags, and you can hear the continuous rustling of everything that surrounds you here. The rustling addresses you, but it can't hear you at all. You feel frightened by the insensibility of the stark southern landscape. But you don't have to be afraid.

Why had I thought of the steppe as a soft, kindly belly? We spent two days driving from Astrakhan to Moscow. My father was on a route: he was deadheading, driving empty, to bring back *chickies* from Moscow. We were traveling light, but the truck, unaccustomed to lightness, for some reason resisted our easy momentum. Brother, the truck, kept stalling, and something thudded inside it.

The drive was supposed to take a single day but took two. My father was driving me and my lover, Liza. Liza was a small woman, so we put her in the sleeper compartment and hid her behind a curtain when we passed traffic patrols, so it looked like there were only two of us. You aren't allowed to have three people in a MAZ.

Liza was on her way to start at the School of Contemporary Art, but she asked us to drop her off before reaching Moscow, in Ulyanovsk. Someone else was waiting for her there. And I had just enrolled at the Gorky Literary Institute. It was a trip meant to be taken with pride, but instead there was only a fumbling awkwardness.

My father liked the writer Maxim Gorky, and the institute where I was going to study literature was named after him. My father said that Gorky had been a *bosyak*, a vagabond, like everyone else in my father's orbit and like my father himself. Seeing myself as a *bosyachka* was embarrassing; I was ashamed of my poverty, my rootlessness. And the ease with which my father claimed Gorky as one of his own was embarrassing, too. He believed that Gorky had been an honest man of the masses, which was true. In his own mind, Gorky remained a poor man into his old age, never knowing what to do with what he'd made. He only knew how to give it away. My father was the same. He didn't know how live on his own money. He knew how to live on the road.

You'll want to know what that means—living on the road. My father used to say that any self-respecting long-distance trucker could wash himself with a liter-and-a-half bottle of water and a few drops of dish soap. His favorite was Fairy, of course. The grassy liquid smelled pungent and lathered well. He used it to scrub himself, his dishes, and anything else in the truck that needed cleaning. This was the way of his limited, bare-bones existence, and there wasn't any other way. Eat, drink, keep relatively clean, and be on the road.

He'd set a scuffed jerrican on the step of his truck. The can had a steel tap, to avoid wasting any water. You had to nimbly turn the tap and use only a few drops. My father lathered his hands and face thoroughly with Fairy soap, which quickly became a rich, uniform layer of foam. Along his forearms the foam turned gray, then black, from the tarry fuel oil and diesel on his hands.

In the cabin of the truck there was a little berth, covered with a threadbare yellow blanket, where he slept during his routes. The berth was a double, like in a sleeper train car, the idea being that a long-haul trucker should be traveling with a shift-swap partner for aid and entertainment. He'd pull over by the thickets of Russian olive at a truck stop, draw the faded calico curtain made from old bedsheets, and go to sleep. The truck had to be parked with other cars on either side, or a Magnit supermarket refrigerator truck would pull in at night and there would be no sleep, only torment. He drove past stops where refrigerator trucks were parked. Always rattling, those bastards, my father said, and they can't even hear themselves in their soundproof cabins with the AC. And what am I supposed to do? I don't have AC, I have to sleep with the windows open to get some air in here.

It was the three of us making the trip, and we decided to forgo spending the night at a stop, since the next one was still far off. We parked by the roadside. My father asked how we were going to bunk up. There's just two berths but three of us. I said that Liza and I would sleep in the steppe. The bugs will eat you alive, my father protested. I said it would be fine, we'd pull the sleeping bags over our heads. He rummaged around on his berth and gave me a light-colored flannelette blanket to spread on the ground, to cushion our sleep.

In the black night we trudged silently through a steppe that was all aglow in the dark. The steppe glimmered and seemed to be a sea of black, poisonous liquid. It looked like crude oil; it wailed. We walked on, trying to find a decent place to sleep.

But there wasn't a single suitable spot. And the deeper we pressed into the darkness of the steppe, the more its boundlessness frightened us. Every flat stretch of ground turned out to be flecked with tough bunches of gray grass. Finally we got tired of walking and decided to clear a small plot to spend the night.

Liza held a flashlight that continually went out. Its beam collided with little steppe pebbles and mounds, inking the dark shadows in the flashlight's feeble yellow light even darker. They were so black they seemed to be cuts in the surface of the world.

The stars gave little light. The headlights of the truck shone on the road. Our shadows were frightening and separate. I dropped to my knees and started tossing away the larger stones, then spread the thin flannelette blanket and laid my sleeping bag on top of it. We got into our sleeping bags, but it was hard to lie there as rocks and hard clusters of steppe sand dug into my back. Still, I said nothing, thinking that if I let Liza see I was uncomfortable, she would never let me live down my weakness. Liza was quiet, too. I don't know if it hurt her to lie on that thin blanket. We weren't speaking to each other. There was nothing to talk about. We were just together.

We lay silently in the dark steppe night. There was nothing around us, only the truck rattling somewhere in the distance; my father was still awake. I could hear the satisfied whoops that generally accompanied his washing up before bed. The steppe carried the sound of his voice and the noise of passing cars. It carried the light chittering of crickets. Something popped by my ear. I turned my head and saw an enormous bug. The bug was oily brown and hard, frantically running its legs along the waterproof headrest of my sleeping bag. Its legs kept skidding on the dark-blue material, and the bug flailed helplessly, like a merry little rowboat fighting against the tide. I couldn't bear its suffering and flicked it into the grass. Buzzing there, the bug found its bearings after the forced flight and rose slowly above the earth, tracing a circle, then reeling slightly as it sailed away into the dark.

The night chattered and chirred. I lay looking into a sky perforated with the glow of white stars. I didn't have sight enough to take it in; I didn't have body enough to inhale it. The blackness of the sky stared back at me. A cool, clammy palm settled on my forearm. I turned my head, remembering that I was sharing this night with quiet, reserved Liza. She was lying with her eyes closed, and I saw the neat, delicate folds of skin on her eyelids. She was breathing evenly, and then she opened her eyes and rolled onto her side so she could look at me.

Turned toward her, I saw her pale face, its narrow lips and nose. She asked me why we weren't speaking. And I had nothing to say to that.

She put her hand on my belly, then slid it awkwardly beneath my jeans. I caught her hand and moved it away from my stomach.

I've always spoken to the steppe. If I had to urinate in it, I would say, hello, steppe, I've come to pee. That night I whispered words of gratitude into the prickly hummock at the foot of the grasses. The hummock looked like the rear of a great bright bumblebee. It accepted my whispered message, and the sound disappeared somewhere inside it.

The black night sky cooled, and drops of cold morning dew appeared on everything. After that came the tiny flies, waking and setting upon us along with the intolerable morning sunlight. They clung to my face, and my damp skin, glistening with overnight oil, felt even tighter. I wanted to flee from the blinding steppe light, but even stronger was the desire to escape my own skin; it felt unbearable.

I lay there destroyed, my stomach cramping. My light jeans were stained with brown blood. In the night the steppe had taken its fee for my stay.

I opened my eyes. The steppe was tearing into me like some

unstoppable ache. Liza was asleep, and near her head sat the small white skull of a steppe mouse. We hadn't noticed it at night but happened not to crush it. When Liza woke, I showed her the skull. The animal remains drew her attention. She blew off the dust and grass, used her thumb to scrape away sun-bleached bits of flesh and fur. The skull became startlingly white, whiter than the stones and grass all around us. Liza put it away in her fanny pack to sketch later. She stood and stretched, as though her sleep in the steppe had been deep and she was fully restored.

— 3 —

You want to know whether my father knew what Liza and I were to each other. How can I put this? He wasn't a stupid or unfeeling man. He could see that there was something going on between us, and once he walked in on us kissing.

We were lying on the kitchen floor. That's where we slept in my father's apartment. Liza had propped up my head with her shoulder, and I had positioned myself on her narrow chest so I could see her face. So I could smell her breath and touch my cheek to the wing of her narrow nose. She bent her head down and kissed me.

In the bright sunlight we lay there in our underwear and undershirts. You'll ask me what it was like. It was like a crime. Inside me, shame blazed a path for itself, and the path grew wider and wider, until my entire body was a body of shame.

We lay there in the morning light, and her underarm smelled like pale hair. The way wet paper smells. It was all like an interminable, unbearable adolescence that had suddenly sprung up between us. It dragged on and it tormented me. I felt like I couldn't breathe, and I badly wanted to kiss her. My head ached in the harsh red light. My underwear grew damp, and the warm, sticky liquid cooled immediately on the gusset, as though a young Volga fish had died there.

You're asking why I know how a Volga fish, the *vobla*, dies, so I'll tell you. My great-grandfather was a fisherman. Granddad was one of those ancient fishermen whose life nobody remembers, because he himself never talked about his past and lived purely in the present, like any old man. No one knew what he had been in his youth, only that his life had been saved by the Manchurian Operation. During the war, all the men were sent to the Western Front, but my great-grandfather was sent east. He spent the war on the Eastern Front, and when it ended, he came home again. No one else from his village came back from the war, just Granddad and two other boys. They'd been sent east, and that had saved them.

I knew nothing about his life except that he'd fought in the war. Meaning I'd always thought he fought against the Germans. Once, when I was five, he put me on the back of his bicycle and pedaled to the House of Veterans. At the House of Veterans an enormous fan rotated the air, and little flags in a model battle scene fluttered in the indoor breeze. My great-grandfather sat not at the veterans' table but somewhere off to the side, listening to the veterans discuss their urgent affairs. When they began to curse in anger, he shushed them, so they wouldn't speak that way in front of a child.

The battle diorama fascinated me. Green cardboard stood in for grass, and for a hill someone had glued on a mass of cotton dipped in iodine. On this low mound stood a little flag of red silk. Whoever made it had cut a small scrap of kumach cloth from the pretty print of a silk dress or scarf. The hill was surrounded by plastic tanks, and the battlefield was strewn with cockroach shit. The diorama artist had glued everything down with carpenter's glue, and roaches had devoured it.

The veterans treated me to tea, gave me shortbread cookies and berry pie. The veterans at the House of Veterans had all fought in the war against the Germans, but my great-grandfather hadn't fought any Germans—that's why he was still around. The only other remaining veteran of the Manchurian Operation had died before I was born, and Granddad felt misplaced among these heroes of the Great Patriotic War. Yet he went to their meetings regularly, since that was where important community issues were decided and veterans' rations distributed. Granddad didn't participate in any of the debates, just picked up his designated parcels of cookies and cognac and sat on the sidelines, consumed with survivor's guilt.

When I grew tired of playing, I sat on the linoleum by his feet and picked at the aluminum clips he used to hold up the hems of his pants. I asked him why he did that, and he told me that if the bike chain got his pants dirty, my great-grandmother would be upset with him. I took the clips and studied them. They felt light; they looked like silly cold fish. One clip sat tightly, another less so. I used the looser one to clip my nose until it turned white. When we came home, Granddad left the clips on the frame of his bike, which he stored in a shed.

Sometimes he would put me in the sidecar of his motorcycle and take me fishing. We saw a dead toad once, a corpse that had inflated to the size of a hot plate. We brought my father fishing with us, too. He was young then, and had thick black hair and all his teeth where they're supposed to be. But remind me later, and I'll tell you about my father's body.

So, my father found this toad blown up to the size of a hot plate, picked it up, and called me over. We were trudging through the marshes of the Volga delta. The ground was wet, and our rubber boots sank in the grassy mire. I was curious about the dead toad, so my father held it up over his head. I wanted to come closer, but there was a stream between us too wide for me to jump. My father looked at the toad, then at me, and then, laughing, cocked his arm and sent the toad flying into the bushes. You'll ask what the toad was like, and I can tell you: it was gray, dead, and enormous.

Before fishing, Granddad would take his shovel and we would head toward the fence, where behind the well lay a damp stretch of unclaimed land. That was the best spot for worms, because the hose was always leaking, and in the shade of the neighbor's poplars the soil there never dried. Granddad dug, and I squatted, tucking my skirt between my thighs, and gathered bits of worms into a little plastic pill bottle. The worms writhed. Everyone used to think that a worm chopped into several pieces goes on living, but that's not true. Did you know that doesn't happen? The chopped worms die, that's all.

We walked along a wood-plank path, past peach and apple trees, toward the southern banya, near which stood twelve of Granddad's sheds. Granddad opened the sheds every morning;

he had a special little cord on which he kept the keys to the padlocks. Inside the sheds it smelled like salt and cured fish, like paper, like grass and dust. Thin filaments of light danced in the darkness, filtering in through the narrow cracks between warped boards. There was Granddad's barrel of large-grained gray salt flecked with black, and a wooden case in which he kept short bracing sticks for gutted *vobla*. Everything smelled like fish and halted time.

From one of the sheds we would take a little homemade fishing pole for me, a larger pole for Granddad, and a sack of nets. Granddad had a long wooden needle he threaded with impeccably white capron thread, which he used for repairs. He'd sit on a tall log, back to the garden and face toward the dark doorways of the sheds, and sing quietly, patching a fishing net.

I loved my great-grandfather, liked trimming the long curly tufts of hair in his ears and nose. In the evenings we would lie on the floor on a red satin quilt and watch *Field of Wonders* and *Name That Tune* on TV. Granddad liked making fun of the host, Valdis Pelšs, calling him Vanka-Vstanka, like the roly-poly toy. I was amazed by his equanimity, his life where everything had its proper place. In the afternoons, after eating a heavy lunch, he went into his cool bedroom to rest. It was then forbidden to make noise in the house. It was best to stretch out on the floor by Granddad's bed, with its metal knobs, and listen to him snore. He slept, and his light checkered shirt stirred at the shoulder. Edging through the closed shutters, a white ray of light fell on his open palm, and a pair of swallows could be heard squabbling in the cherry tree near the fence.

And so Granddad would collect the two fishing poles, the

nets, a little canvas bag of bread, the bottle of pink worms, and an aluminum case of fishing tackle. He'd sit me in the sidecar of his red motorcycle, and we would drive to the ferry crossing.

The brownish water roiled by the ferry churned, and I peered into it as though something important would surely surface: an enormous fish, or the body of a drowned man.

On a little pier, Granddad and I sat waiting for something to bite. When the tense, silent movements of a hungry fish that had bitten the morsel of worm on my hook tugged at the line, I cut it and pulled up a gray shining *vobla* or rudd. The fish thrashed in my hands as I nimbly withdrew the sharp, thin hook from its sticky, trembling mouth.

Having caught the fish, Granddad and I decided its fate. If it was a large fish, we'd drop it into our scuffed, light-colored pail of murky river water. If it was a young fish, we'd throw it back in the river, so it could live awhile longer.

By midday the water in the pail grew warm, and the big *vobla*, already weakened, died in the heat. The cold fish, with its metallic shine, became slimy all over. The slime was also cold; it had a salty reek of blood and iodine.

Such is the smell of shame. Such is the smell of my shame. Everyone has their own shame, and this is the smell of mine: rosy fish blood, iodine, dried apples. Now I'll ask you—what does yours smell like? In the orange shadows of the summer kitchen, on a sofa tidily covered with a green quilt, I showed the neighbor girl Nastya what I had between my legs. We were identical children. Skinny, happy, wearing white jersey underwear. But between my legs I had a hole. It was always leaking and demanding to be filled. It was like the scuffed pail of murky river water. It smelled of salt, and there was salt shining on the sides of the gray fish. The garland of fish glimmered in the hot, still air of the summer kitchen. The innards of the fish, held open by Granddad's bracing sticks, were still fresh and pink, like my vulva.

Nastya stared into me without looking away. I hadn't removed my underwear completely, just lifted my butt, pulled it down to my knees, and sat, parting my legs as wide as possible. Nastya was looking inside me, and I, a five-year-old, was stirred by an ardent excitement at the possibility of showing myself like this. I had shown myself to the other girls at kindergarten, too, and they had let me look at them. One of them let me feel between her legs—she was pink and smelled sour, disturbing me.

The rays of deep sunset light breaking through the kitchen curtains became tough, tender little feelers. Irrepressible, they stroked my body.

Then Nastya said she wanted to play family. She drew close to my face and threw her whole body on top of mine. I was looking into her eyes, and her suntanned face was calm. She wore the placid expression of a person who spends long hours working at something she can do perfectly.

The thick, sour smell was everywhere. The smell was me, and it was sweet to feel at one with it. Her body made me warm. The closeness of her body made me warm. The entirety of space had transformed into this physical closeness, and the whole world had turned out to be one with my little body.

My father was coming to call us to have fish pie. The pie was made with the pike my great-grandfather had pulled up in his net that morning, while the rest of us were sleeping. He brought the pike back alive, covered in slime and dark tendrils of seaweed. My father was walking over the spoiled fallen apples, past frogs accidentally trampled to death, past the pumpkin patch bathed in dying August light. He was walking through clover and ripe, meaty plantain grass. Everything bowed and bent beneath his stride, and when he lifted his foot, it straightened and looked just the same again. Limp in anticipation of the evening dew, the greenery rustled and squeaked beneath his feet.

Everything around me was green. Everything around me was golden. I was gold. I didn't hear him coming. I missed the creak of the opening door. Over Nastya's shoulder, I saw my father's head as he told us it was time for pie. He was looking somewhere above us. Nastya pulled away from me. Her pristine white undershirt had ridden up in the tussle and now dropped down to cover her taut stomach.

My father waited for us in the kitchen doorway. He was playing with the threadbare fringe of the window curtains. We rose from the quilt and fixed our white undershirts, and I pulled my underwear back up. We walked toward the garden, where everyone had gathered around the table to eat pie. My father was in a good mood; he showed us the hedgehog's bowl, from which the animal had pilfered all the cherry pits and scarlet crayfish shells. Then he pointed out the hedgehog, crossing a distant strawberry patch.

We waited for night to come, so we could hear the chirring of the crickets and the light click of the hedgehog's nails on the painted boards of the porch. We waited for night to come, and my shame was bitter, like the pike's amber-colored roe.

Now we lay on the kitchen floor, and Liza's armpit smelled like pale hair. I wasn't a five-year-old girl, and my father wasn't a robust thirty-year-old man. Everything had changed. He was faded and awfully aged for his years, and his hard head, dark-haired in his youth, looked like a scrap of soaked butcher paper. The symmetry of his face had flown, and white spit collected and clung in the corner of his lips that didn't move when he smiled.

The light was too strong. It poured into the kitchen through the transparent tulle of the curtains and flooded everything: the gas stove, the rickety table covered with a worn vinyl tablecloth, the washing machine. The light fell also on the floor where we writhed in our morning agitation. It smelled like dusty carpet and the greasy smear on the side of the refrigerator.

The skin at the tip of Liza's nose had turned pink in yesterday's sunlight. She passed the back of her hand over my lips, and I smelled paint; it mingled with the scents of sweat, dust, and grease. Time slowed. I had no desire to get up. I didn't want to do anything that would interrupt our mute lingering.

But the morning went on; my father woke in the next room and turned on the TV. The TV began to wail, devouring the silence. The light shifted, altering the nature and density of things.

In the tiny rented apartments where my father lived, personal boundaries did not exist. The locks on the bathroom doors didn't work, because wooden doors expand in damp and then can't close all the way. You had to tie a special rag to the doorknob to keep the door shut while you were bathing or using the toilet. People get all mixed up in these kinds of apartments; folks who are strangers to one another come together to live a forced communal life. My father got together with a woman like this—not out of love, but convenience and desperation. Every man needed a woman who waited for him, who cooked, cleaned, and met his sexual needs. They rented a one-room apartment and lived there together when he was home from his trucking routes. For a little while, I lived with them, too. And when Liza came, space was found for her. We lived together, the four of us: some people who didn't really know one another and a skinny calico cat.

I told Liza that my father was awake and asked her to move away from me, so he wouldn't see how close we were. Liza said that we could lie around for a while longer, he was still watching TV. But my father had already come into the kitchen. With the shrieking TV we hadn't heard him rise from the sofa and stride quickly over the carpet squares that had been laid out to form a walkway.

My father paused in the doorframe, watching our brief kiss. He might as well have been looking straight through us. As though behind our heads, lips, noses, hair, there was something else that had drawn his attention. I saw his glittering eyes beneath their drooping eyelids. One eyebrow sagged, as did the immobile corner of his mouth. I moved away from Liza and smiled at him. He told me to make him eggs and brew the coffee.

I got up, took my shorts from a stool draped with a knitted cover, and put them on. Cold enveloped me; it was impossible to breathe. I indicated to Liza with a look that she should put away our bedding. But Liza didn't get the message. She lay there looking me up and down playfully with her cool gray eyes. Liza didn't like my father, whereas my father didn't care about her one way or the other. She was just another mouth to eat the things we bought with the money he made.

Sometimes my father would ask Liza a question. He asked her why she shaved her head, or what artists lived on. She replied reluctantly. She considered my father a drone and a fool. When Liza was drawing he'd peek at her work and click his tongue, saying that it looked just like the real thing. He asked her to draw Brother, his truck, but Liza didn't take commissions. She was making art.

I was ashamed of Liza in front of my father. Ashamed of her thoughtlessness, her unwillingness to try to make herself useful and comprehensible to a grown man. And I was ashamed of my father in front of Liza. Ashamed of his plainness and his fustiness, his rough edges. He was like an old raccoon, ravaged by ticks and disease. He wasn't good at expressing how he felt.

I was always ashamed of my father.

When I say that we were strangers, I'm telling you the truth. My father was a complete stranger to me, really a stranger. He was as solitary as a boulder in the road. You can see a boulder, you can touch it. But you can't say anything to it, or if you do, it'll hear you, but it won't reply.

There's no reciprocation in this world—I'm used to that. The world is a rock garden. My father's solitude disappointed me. He disappointed me. But he enchanted me, too, with his solitude.

It was the difficult summer of 2010. He met me in the square by the train station in Vladimir. I recognized him right away. I had last seen him in 2000, at the station in Astrakhan. He got there moments before our train departed, though he'd promised to drive my mother and me to the station. She was smoking anxiously by the train when he appeared, and I watched him from the window of the train car. The scorching Astrakhan sun was shining; it bent everything living toward the earth and made everything dead even more so. My mother was standing in that sun.

Her tanned skin glistened. My father came to her meekly, wearing a blissful smile. He'd brought a sack of some useless sweets and a bundle of dried fish.

He was completely destroyed. His body went on living its steady life, but his face seemed to be both asleep and awake in some other dimension, inaccessible to us. It wasn't the first summer he'd spent on heroin. I don't know when he finally stopped shooting up, but since that day in Astrakhan I hadn't seen him for ten years. He may have stopped when his courtyard buddy, the one who bought and shot up with him, died a terrible death. No one explained to me how the man had died. He just died, that's all.

My father had always done drugs. When my mother was out, he closed the door and sealed the gap at the bottom with a towel, so that I, his four-year-old daughter, wouldn't smell the *khimka*—cannabis cooked in solvent. But I could smell it anyway as I sat watching tapes on our stolen VCR. I had a tape about two dogs and a Siamese cat who spoke in human voices. My stoned father and his friends thought this was hilarious. I thought it was funny, too; I wanted to please the grown-ups with my great sophistication.

In the early, overcast morning my father stood in the square by the Vladimir train station. Everything there looked dull. Fires were burning outside the city, and dense, heavy smog hung in the windless air. My father wore a short-sleeved half-buttoned shirt, baggy cotton pants, and black slides on his bare feet. He was holding a small plastic bag, knotted shut. His dark forehead glistened in the scant sunlight breaking through the smoke.

I still have to tell you about my father's body; I haven't forgotten, it just isn't time yet.

I went to him, and he greeted me with a meager hug. He looked at me the way parents look at adult children they didn't know or see while they were growing up. Putting his hands on my shoulders, trying to be friendly, he voiced his surprise at how big I'd gotten. I was twenty then. I wasn't *big*—I had just grown up.

He asked if I was hungry. We walked to the station café and ordered fried eggs sunny side up, tomato salad, and two coffees. Fat brown granules of instant coffee stuck to the side of my plastic cup, and I kept failing to scrape them off with the useless white stirrer. This was a good reason to be quiet. I didn't know what to say to my father, and he was silently blowing on his own coffee to cool it down. He always cooled his hot drinks so he could drink them lukewarm. I saw myself reflected in that habit.

Our resemblance was obvious. I was a gawky, slightly pigeon-toed twenty-year-old woman. His gait was similarly awkward. I looked into his eyes, and he looked back at me with my own aged, time-blasted eyes. His mouth was my mouth, only toothless. He hadn't stopped being my father over the decade we hadn't seen each other. He'd led his own separate life for a long time, but the stuff of which he was made was identical to mine. This morning I looked at myself in the mirror and saw that my eyelids are gradually beginning to sag. They look like worn-out canvas. My deep-set eyes are even closer now to the eyes I saw at the train station café in Vladimir.

When we finished our coffees, I asked where he'd left his car, and he grimaced old-mannishly, saying that oversize vehicles weren't allowed in the city. Brother was parked at a long-distance truck stop beyond the bypass road. He said that we needed to buy a camera. Everything around us was shrouded in dry smoke. Central Russia was smoldering and charging the air with an ugly, suffocating haze.

We left the café and lit cigarettes. I couldn't see why we needed a camera, but I felt too self-conscious to ask. My father hailed a cab, and we drove to an Eldorado electronics store. It's strange, I think about this all the time, but I've never gotten past it. There are so many different places in this world, and they stay exactly where we leave them. Everything can change in a given place, things can break down, but I assure you—the place itself will remain. It stays behind when we leave, and it's still there when we come back again. The circumstances in a place may change so that you're no longer able to get to it—someone could take over, build a border. But what's worse is that you may not be able to return because you've died. And death, as you know, is when everything remains except for you. While a place persists into the future, painlessly. With supreme indifference.

That Eldorado store is still exactly where we left it. You know that kind of spot, a slightly shabby discount emporium. I found out that it's still there when my wife and I were visiting Vladimir and waiting for a pizza shop to open. It was a March morning, light rain, hot in the sun and still cold in the shade. I watched a black puddle of melting snow expanding on the asphalt. Everything sparkled; it was spring. I looked up to get a sense of where we were and saw the dilapidated Eldorado. It was the same one where my father and I had bought a little black Olympus camera for two thousand five hundred rubles, along with a memory card.

I'd been surprised, back then, that the memory card cost half as much as the camera itself.

My father silently passed me the bag with the camera and looked over what I was wearing. I had on thick jeans and sneakers. That's no good, my father said, it's hot out, and the closer we get to Astrakhan, the hotter it'll be. He caught another cab, and we drove to the market.

I'd come to visit my father because I needed to see him. My mother said that he was a *fucking slacker* and accused me of being just like him. I'd always thought of my father as less of a father than a brother. But in any case, he was a strange man with whom I was supposed to get into a truck and travel—not because I wanted to but because he said so. I was doing everything now that he said I had to: I had to insert the memory card into the camera and take a picture of him by the Andrei Rublev statue. After that, I had to stand by the statue myself and smile while he took my picture.

In the photograph I'm wearing short shorts in a green-and-white Hawaiian print. My father bought them for me at the market in Vladimir. He walked for a long time past stands piled with cheap, noxious-smelling clothes, until finally stopping across from one of the kiosks. I stopped next to him, and we were immediately approached by a wiry saleswoman in a pink cap bedazzled with dull little rhinestones. At my father's request, she used a wooden stick with a hook to pull down a pack of multicolored shorts. All the shorts looked vulgar to me, but my father insisted that I choose a pair from these particular options. Compared to the pink, violet, and orange-blue ones, the green-and-white shorts seemed the most modest, so I chose them. From his breast pocket, my father drew several bills, soft with sweat, and paid two hundred fifty rubles.

Now I had to immediately take off the thick jeans and change into my new shorts. My father insisted, so I undressed behind a wooden counter strewn with T-shirts depicting Putin and printed with dumb jokes about beer and the Russian character. My father noticed a shirt with a sloppy print of Putin riding a bear, aiming a rifle, and charging right at us across wind-thrown trees. He found the shirt amusing. He stabbed at it with his stubby finger, and I saw that every single one of his fingernails was darkly outlined in fuel oil. Oil had worked its way into the ridges of his skin. His clothes smelled like diesel, and his shirt and shorts showed the rough white stains of salty sweat. My father's body was like a sunless salt marsh—taut and covered in scars, salt, and black oil. It had aged before its time. He burst out laughing at a joke printed on one of the shirts, and I saw deep ruts of wrinkles form by his sunken eyes. His mouth was dark; he had barely any teeth.

Standing there on trampled cardboard, I saw that my father had grown irrevocably old. He didn't look like a forty-three-year-old man, he looked like a seventy-year-old geezer. Everything about him was heavy. He was like an old tree struck by lightning, fallen across the path. I couldn't tear my eyes away, even as I tried to avoid looking at him.

In the narrow passage between the counter and a plastic chair, I could feel that the heat and smoke were making my body swollen and clammy. In my new shorts, I felt indecently exposed among these mountains of cheap synthetic crap. My father was still laughing; he told me to follow him and I went, folding my jeans into the bag from Eldorado and feeling my damp thighs rubbing against each other.

— **5** —

I remember the drab endless steppe, and the damp Volga delta, and the murky yellow Bakhtemir River. Do you know what the water of the Bakhtemir was like? It was as thick as the silt stirred up from the river bottom. Ferries sailed by; boats sailed by. Fish swam and thumped against the riverbed. The calm yellow Bakhtemir ran into the Caspian Sea.

I walked into the river near the pier, pinched my nose, shut my eyes, and floated on the yellow waves. Can you imagine what I heard? I heard the water flowing along the silty riverbed. The water was greater than all else, and it screeched like an old, furious chain. It scared me and I stood up, and a shard of black seashell scratched the sole of my foot. The water in my eyes made everything blurry, like the iridescent inside of a mussel shell. Sunlight struck the surface of the waves, but the water leached away light and warmth; the riverbed was cold. The fine sunbleached hairs on my arms were plastered with sand and dark river grass, and wafting over from somewhere came the stench of decaying seaweed.

———

I know nothing else about those parts. I only know that the land is very fertile. Black mole crickets devour a vine of oxheart tomatoes. At night, in the cool dew, a sweet apricot bursts, undone by its own ripeness. Everything swells in the humidity. The scratch on my foot kept getting infected and took a while to heal. I had to braid my hair tightly to keep it from catching on a piece of driftwood or tangling in seaweed.

Once Granddad pulled up a tangle of water chestnuts in his net and gave me the spiny brown nuts. We didn't eat them; Granddad brought them back as little fishing souvenirs. While wet, a chestnut glistened like the head of a fantastic beetle, and drying, it came to look more like thick hide. The chestnut was prickly, with a gloomy odor of mud. The seashells there were brittle. The receding tide left the shore bare, and it stood strewn with the little white, gray, and turquoise eyes of seashells. I walked along the sand collecting them—cone-shaped, scalloped—into a durable plastic bag. When the bag was full, I tied it to my belt, got on Granddad's motorcycle, hugged him around the middle, and heard my seashells cracking between us. At home, we shook the shards of my shells onto the floor of the chicken coop, so the white and orange laying hens could peck at them. The shards were light blue and delicate as fragile moonstone, but their blues quickly drowned in the thick chicken droppings.

And that's all; I don't remember anything else. I wrote to someone I knew at the Falanster bookstore, asking him to dig up whatever they had on Astrakhan. He found a reference book for me: *Speaking Astrakhan: Vocabulary, Figurative Language, Proverbs,*

Texts. The book was so old that the booksellers had to paste a label on the spine and write the title in blue pen, and they apologized for the state of the book as they were ringing it up. But what I care about are the letters.

My father also used to say that the most important thing was having some letters to look at. Every morning, he stopped the truck by a newspaper kiosk and availed himself of the day's papers: *Arguments and Facts*, *Express Gazette*, and always the local paper, like the *Volgograd Pravda*.

He read the papers after lunch, sprawled on his berth and chewing a greasy matchstick. He read them during lunch, too, holding them open on the steering wheel, scanning page after page. I don't know how much he really retained of what he was reading, since he was simultaneously eating and listening to a Mikhail Krug tape. In his time as a long-haul trucker, he'd lost practically all the hearing in his left ear, so he listened to the radio at full volume in order to make out every word and chuckle at every one of the hosts' witticisms.

I studied my father, a complete stranger to me. I watched him eat and sleep, trying to hold his image in mind in order to understand who he really was and how he had turned out to be my father. But I couldn't do it. My father did not fit, and he filled me with confusion and dread.

As a onetime heroin user, my father still planned little benders for himself. On those days he didn't go out but simply shut himself up in his apartment, or settled down somewhere with a few other truckers and very quickly got wasted. The other men knew this habit of his and afterward would bring him home in his own gray hatchback, three of them ferrying him inside. In those moments his small, muscled body sagged heavily, and three strong men struggled to lift him from the *tapchan*, load him into the back seat, and drive him home in a three-car caravan. They pulled him out by the building entrance and as a trio trundled him to the fifth floor. At home, my slightly sobered father would wander the apartment like a ranging bear. Sometimes he fell, tripping on the rug, cursing loudly, and stumbling back up again. Having wandered to his heart's content, he went to bed and spent the night howling in his sleep. I don't know what he saw in his dreams, but he cried out and whimpered like an old, exhausted dog.

And then, in the morning, he woke up absolutely refreshed. As though inside him there were a gaping dark maw that the night before had been thrown the thing it craved and had since closed up completely, gone without a trace. Relaxed, he'd go pick up a few beers, then while away the afternoon on the sofa by the TV. For lunch he ate fatty soup and drank sour kefir, then lay dozing on the sofa, twirling the minute hairs by his belly button with one hand and guarding the remote control with the other. The television roared continuously, and as my father snored I made a few attempts to lower the volume. But as soon as the sound died down, he would open his eyes, turn toward me with his functioning ear, and ask me not to turn off the box.

By evening, when the reek of the night's vodka and the morning's hair of the dog had faded, my father got in his little car, as he called his Lada Nine hatchback, and drove to end the day on the Volga embankment. He wove through the festive crowd like a fish through the bulrushes. The crowd was unreal and unknowable to him, it was incomprehensible, but he knew how to get through it. Standing by the musical fountains, for a long time he watched the violet lights, humming as he swayed a little to the beat of the canned music. The fountain didn't impress him, but it cheered him with its frivolity.

I kept wondering who the city was trying to please with these vapid displays, the piddling singing fountains and little statues of ladies with lapdogs and fat guys on benches with their bellies rubbed to a high shine. In Nizhny Novgorod, on the Pokrovka, its high street, there's a sculpture of the Bully Goat from the fairy tale, its polished back glinting in the sun. People are constantly plunking their kids down on the goat or trying to climb up on it themselves. The surrounding fountains meanwhile play an instrumental version of Ace of Base's "Beautiful Life," but over the roar of the falling water and the noise of conversation nothing can be heard but the squeak of the highest notes. The fountain my father visited was meant to delight, and although it was plainly absurd, its presence alone obliged him to be happy. And so my father was happy. And the people around him were happy, too, snapping pictures of the singing fountain with their smartphones.

My father asked if I'd brought the camera, and I told him I hadn't.

There you go again. He sighed, disappointed. We could've gotten a shot of the fountain.

I found my little Nokia in my pocket and told my father I could take a picture with my phone, then send it to my computer or print it, if we wanted. He perked up and immediately went to pose. I toggled over to my phone's camera and looked at the screen. A violet blur shone in the blue-blackness of the Astrakhan night. Adjacent to the blur I could make out the contours of my father's gray shirt and the silhouette of his round brown head, the glare of the diode streetlamps bouncing off his forehead. But the whole picture was somehow wrong; there was no joy in it. I took the shot and went over to my father. It's not really coming out, I said. It's too dark, my phone camera isn't good enough. My father looked at the picture and burst out laughing at its ridiculousness. In his laughter I could hear his disappointment at a missed opportunity.

It's all right, he said. Next time don't forget the camera, and we'll get a picture of us by the fountain.

At a shooting gallery he handed the boy working the tent a hundred-ruble bill and picked up a rifle. Clearing his throat, he took aim and hit three cans out of five. The dull metal balls thunked against the empty cans, and my rejoicing father raised both fists to the sky, shook them, and howled. The boy appraised my father's shooting and presented him with a little plush Mickey Mouse key chain. My father toyed with the key chain briefly, then passed it to me. Filled with shame and pity, I accepted his trophy. He didn't know how to treat me like an adult; for him, I was still a little girl. At the ice cream tent he bought a wafer cone for me and two bottles of beer, one for each of us. I watched him, still trying to understand what he, being the person he was, felt about my being there with him. The Volga flowed slowly; by day's end it looked glassy and mute. After I hooked the key chain to my keys, the stuffing began spurting out of it, and I felt even more miserable. Everything my father did, every single thing he said or accomplished, was all like this pathetic synthetic key chain. We drank our beers in silence, and then my father called his friend Kolyan to drive us home in the Lada Nine.

My father loved to tell the story of going to Saint Petersburg a few times at the very start of his long-distance career. While in the area, he'd had time to stop by Peterhof and get his picture taken with an actress dressed as a lady-in-waiting and a tall actor sporting a fake Peter the Great mustache. In the photo, he's standing in front of a fountain, one hand brushing the lady's impeccably white satin glove and the other grasping the handle of Peter's cane. He's wearing a clean, ironed beige T-shirt and fresh linen slacks, a pack of Bond cigarettes peeking out of his zippered breast pocket, and the shape of the pocket reveals that along with his smokes my father also keeps a roll of bills in there. And that is all he has: someone else's truck left at a stop near the bypass and a roll of bills for the road. You can see the creases in his clothes, ironed and packed away during the drive. He'd kept this outfit in the cabinet beneath his berth, bringing it from Astrakhan to Petersburg to wear on his day off and go have a look at the grand Peterhof Palace. He's smiling for the picture, and I can see the pride in his face. He's surrounded by luxury and grandeur. My father's body, wedged into this context, looks more like a wreck. He's only a stagehand, and soon the curtain will rise, and the powdered lady and her companion will live the life of the aristocratic elite, so that other people can behold all that beauty and feel proud to have some part in the magnificent proceedings. My father said he paid a hundred rubles for the photo and threw in another fifty for a copy. He gave both photographs to his mother, my grandmother, as a memento.

My father said that he used to have a habit of going on benders during long stops in the steppe. I was there for a few of these. We stood waiting for pipe by Kapustin Yar for nearly a week, and at the Rybinsk Reservoir we were stopped for three days. My father told me that he drove his routes alone to save more money. A partner came at a cost—you had to feed him and pay him, and meanwhile his only use was keeping an eye on the truck while you slept.

About five years earlier, my father had drunk himself half to death waiting in a queue to load more cargo near Volgograd. He passed out and came to on the roadside. No truck, no documents. Wearing just his shorts and plastic slides. The truck was never his in the first place, and to ransom it he'd have needed five hundred thousand rubles—and where was he supposed to get that much money when the tractor alone eats up fifteen thousand in fuel going one way and on the Volgograd route the suspension is always blowing out, too.

He walked to the truck stop, talked to a couple of guys there. They gave him a lift to the next stop. A tractor trailer isn't a needle in a haystack. If your truck gets stolen, you're going to find it no matter what. It's big, it's slow, there are only so many roads it can take. By noon, my father had come to the stop where his MAZ truck was parked. The cargo was still there, everything was still where it was supposed to be, only none of it was in my father's possession at the moment. He found the people who had stolen the truck and talked to them. And something helped him get back both the truck and the cargo. Most likely it was his criminal past, the language of which he remembered well. He didn't drink on his routes after that if he was driving alone, just at home and after unloading.

— 6 —

Can the earth understand the glyphs of the seeds
planted in it by the sower?

— VELIMIR KHLEBNIKOV

And when the cops are at your door
The animals croak, the milk goes sour . . .

— KASPIYSKIY GRUZ

My father loved the music of Mikhail Krug. He loved those songs the way some women love con men. A woman stripped down to her last stitch of clothing will deny to the end that she's been had. She'll go on believing in the myth she's been fed and hoping for her happy ending. And so my father lived by the principles proposed by Krug, not least because they aligned perfectly with his own view of the world.

Khlebnikov, the poet, wrote:

They say that the songs of labor can only be written by those who labor at machines. Can this be true? Isn't the essence of song a departure from the self, from one's everyday activity? Is a song not an escape from oneself? . . . Without a flight from the self, there would be no space to wander. Inspiration has always belied the origins of the singer. Medieval knights eulogized simple shepherds; Lord Byron chose pirates; the Buddha, a prince, praised poverty. Similarly, Shakespeare, tried for theft, speaks the language of kings, as does the modest burgher's son Goethe. Their art is concerned with courtly life. In the tundra of Pechorsky Krai, which has never known war, the oral epics of Vladimir and his warriors live on, long forgotten on the Dnepr.

Extending this line of thought, I'll add that the musicians Mikhail Krug, Vladimir Vysotsky, and Aleksandr Rozenbaum have never been to prison, that the rapper Shilo from Krovostok never fought or killed anyone, and that the guys in the band Kaspiyskiy Gruz never bumped anyone off or sold drugs.

The nature of an era is such that it ends, and people are left to live out their lives on their own, stranded in the future. My mother lived like that after she lost her job. She'd spent twenty-five years at a factory, and after moving to a different city she found herself helpless and superfluous to her time and place. The factory had processed my mother and her youth like so much raw material, without giving her any idea of how to live in the future. And she herself, enamored with her youth and strength, seemed to be stuck back there, in the past, redundant even to herself.

Let me give you another example. You've seen Goya's *Saturn*

Devouring His Son? The painting is often compared to Rubens's painting of the same name, but Rubens's Saturn is calm, biting meditatively into the belly of a child. This is the way elderly people eat, unhurried, deep in concentration. But Goya's Saturn is mad—see his eyes? They glitter in the dark. He starts with the head, and we see the headless body sagging in his grasp. That is the image of an epoch. It consumes you, starting with the head, because people can be identified by their faces. Saturn devours the head in order to erase every individual feature. Time wipes away all distinctions, even the distinction of sex—in Goya's painting, the son hangs with his back to the viewer, and we see a bloodied white body without knowing whether it's male or female. And Saturn, the gaunt, crazed old man, looks more like a woodland spirit or a demon, emerging from the dark. Looking at Goya's painting, I can hear the crunching of bones and the tearing of flesh. And I hear a terrifying howl. The sound is coming from Saturn himself: he moans like a ghost haunting an old castle, he whines like a mangy dog, he roars as he chews. As I look at the painting, he begins to stand out toward me, and his painted body becomes perceptible and real. I know that it's me hanging there, in his veined, gnarled hands.

At school, in biology class, we played a game we called *cartoons*. In the corner of a page of my notebook, I'd draw the rudimentary stick figure of a person; on the next page the person changed positions. You could curl the page around your pencil and angle it to make the drawing move. Kids who were better artists could manage not just a few different poses but a whole animated world. A dog ran through that world, a flower bloomed, a man went to bed, a bottle shattered. All that motion, development, and destruction depended on the speed of your paging through. When pages stuck together a whole phase could disappear, making for something pretty close to a montage sequence. You could also grow your flower very slowly, as is appropriate to the concept of a flower. Nobody sees a flower grow, it blooms unnoticed. My father, once a Young Pioneer, planted a row of poplar trees behind our house. The saplings grew tall and gave a lot of shade in the mornings, but I could never understand how a tree managed to grow when no one ever saw it happening. Maybe the growth goes unnoticed because a tree, standing out in the heat, wind, and sun, is always rustling its leaves and branches, distracting the human eye from its gradual ascent? In real life, we can see that everything that falls, falls quickly, and the moment of disintegration is even harder to capture. What our game allowed us to do was slow down any event that usually happens quickly—our falling bottles could break at very slow speed. With the cartoon game, we could make any process accessible and reversible.

But here's what I'm trying to tell you. The hand that controls the speed of the shift moves quickly, quicker and quicker each turn. Such is the function of time. In the eighties, the criminal system of worldviews and hierarchies that had developed in the Soviet labor camps—the system of the *blatniye*—spilled out beyond the camps and came to the role previously held by the weakening Soviet government. When things start happening and you play some not entirely insignificant part in the proceedings, you tend to think it'll last forever. People think this way when they gain even a little power, it doesn't matter how that power was won. But time gallops on and seems to speed up with every step. The *blatniye* weren't in charge for long; another set of criminals came to replace them. Time's maw snapped shut, leaving some of them laid out in sumptuous caskets in the cemeteries. Others leaped out, to live their lives in the future. My father was one of these. He left Ust-Ilimsk in 1999 to dodge a felony charge. I don't know whether this is true, but it's what my mother told me: he passed out in somebody's apartment after a bender and woke up at the police station being tortured. Someone had stolen everything they could carry from that apartment, and so my father, with a single bag containing a toothbrush and a change of underwear, fled to Astrakhan. The reason he wound up in Ust-Ilimsk in the first place I'll explain later, when it comes up.

But now, the *blatniye*.

In their criminal hierarchy he held the rank of foot soldier. There were a lot of others like him: taxi drivers, working guys, men who hadn't spent very long in prison and didn't think of the *blatnoy* way of life as a default. My father had a car, which fed him and gave his life meaning. My great-grandfather had taught him to drive; in the village of Trudfront, near Astrakhan, he put my father behind the steering wheel of a tractor and showed him how to start it up. One summer break when he was twelve, my father stole Granddad's tractor and was whipped with a leather belt with a star-shaped buckle. He did his mandatory army service in Mongolia, where he drove a dump truck and went three hundred kilometers through the desert to find moonshine during Gorbachev's anti-alcohol campaign. He was highly valued for that. He was a true member of the collective, he served the collective in everything—delivering moonshine was no exception.

He knew how to negotiate, and he knew how to survive. My mother said that in Ust-Ilimsk every dog knew him. And that was true, everyone did know us—people said hello to us in the streets; they grew quiet when my mother came to stand in queues for hard-to-get roly-poly toys. Remember those roly-polies? I had two, a big one and a small one, crimson and baby blue, and when they wobbled they emitted a strange metallic sound. The sound was supposed to amuse and delight.

My father was only a foot soldier in the ranks of the *blatniye*—or so it was generally thought. But I don't really believe that anymore. After he got out of prison he came home again, but he never slept there. My mother said he'd stop by in the mornings to drop off money and goods. On the balcony off the foyer of our apartment sat cases of vodka and cigarettes. He left stacks of bills on the shelves, though there wasn't much to spend them on—you had to stand in line for everything. When videocassette recorders and imported televisions appeared in the city, my father brought home a color LG TV wrapped in an old blanket. It was followed by a VCR and a Dendy game system.

I had a toy stroller for my doll and a fancy little sheepskin coat. The neighbor girls hated me for this and called me a spoiled little rich girl, and I felt ashamed of having things while others didn't. It's possible that the girls' resentment was not entirely their own, but also their parents' resentment of who my father was. Their parents were honest doctors and factory workers. My father was a criminal, and in our idle home the money never ran out, and this was unfair. One day the girls stopped me in the street to ask if they could look into my stroller. Inside the stroller lay my fancy doll. They exchanged glances and asked politely if they could take Masha the doll for a walk, and, trusting in their goodwill, I relinquished the handle of the stroller to one of them. Then the girls, cackling like little furies, sent my stroller careening down the road. Its white rubber wheels jumped as they hit the potholes in the pavement, and I could hear my Masha bouncing around inside. The girls ran down the road in the quiet, bright day, laughing. Disillusioned, I sat down on a bench beneath a poplar tree. I wasn't sorry I had shared my toys with them, but I felt sorry for Masha, who had suffered the effects of their hatred.

One day in the winter of 1994 my mother came to pick me up from kindergarten. She didn't rush me and didn't seem upset; she went about everything the way she always did, with dignity and composure. She passed me my hose and tights, tugged down my flannel skirt, tied on my kerchief, and laced my rabbit-fur hat tightly before we walked out into the cold. By the gates of the kindergarten a police car was waiting for us. My mother said that I shouldn't say anything to the cops, because they wanted to put my father in jail. A fat cop stepped out of the car, picked me up, and swung me into the back; my mother climbed in after. In the panel separating the front from the cage there was a small grate, through which the fat cop winked at me and asked if I was afraid of him. I'm not afraid, I said. My mother sat me on a little faux-leather bench, and we drove home. I could see the ice-shagged treetops through a small grate in the door. They glittered like precious jewels in the dark night. Everything around me was government issue, and the poverty of that world stood out against the white snowbanks and scorched my eyes.

They were already waiting by our building to do the search. My mother said later that the cops were looking for drugs, money, gold jewelry. They weren't interested in electronics— everyone's electronics were stolen then, no one had receipts. I was put in an armchair by the coffee table, and my mother told me to take off my fur coat and wool tights myself. In the meantime, she followed the fat cop around the apartment, providing a running commentary on his actions. She wasn't scared and she wasn't concerned. It's possible that she wasn't afraid because she knew my father would wriggle out of this. She also looked calm because she was angry at him—he hadn't thought to check the lining of a particular stolen hat, and its previous owner had spotted it at the market.

The pretty new mink hat really suited my mother. She wore it with a glittering Lurex scarf. But earlier that day, picking out beef tongue at the market meat counter, she'd felt a commotion at her back. Turning, she saw a disheveled woman in an expensive fur coat pulling a fat cop by the sleeve with one hand, and with the other, pointing emphatically at my mother's hat. The meat counter clerk dried her knife on a clean rag and passed it to the cop. The cop asked for my mother's hat and used the tip of the blade to neatly pull up its silk lining, revealing the owner's phone number, address, and name, written into the leather. He also noted two slits on the hat's sides; at some point an elastic band had been attached to it, in case the hat was taken off on the go. And indeed it had been taken off on the go, as the owner was coming home one night from a birthday party. The thief had had to fight for it, and he kicked the woman; she clutched her stomach and he ran away. My mother wore the hat without any strap because she knew it would not be taken off her. All the thieves in the city knew her by sight, and no one would dare try anything.

And so she was angry at my father's lack of foresight. She was also mad because the cops were tramping in their street shoes over her freshly mopped floors, and meltwater mixed with sand and grime ran from their boots. My mother followed in the fat cop's tracks, kicking along a rag to keep the dirt from spreading. The fat cop rummaged familiarly inside the wardrobe where my toys were kept and upended a box of building blocks onto our flat-woven rug. He groped in the depths of the wardrobe, moving aside the roly-polies and a plastic pyramid toy. He shook out the ironed bed linens from an adjacent drawer and threw them on the sofa. In the bathroom, he lifted the lid of the toilet tank, flinging it back down angrily when he found nothing inside. The porcelain lid cracked, and my mother gathered up the thin shards, like the shells of little freshwater mollusks.

Since I was a little child I'd been told not to talk to cops. My father taught me to hate them but avoid insulting them to their faces. My mother taught me to despise them. It's generally thought that if upon hearing a cop shout "Hey!" in the street you feel compelled to turn around, you live in a police state. In my case it was all a bit different. I was afraid of cops because I was my father's daughter, because they'd rummaged through my toys in my home, acting like they owned the place. Of course, they'd had grounds for doing this; it was their way of restoring order. But their method of restoring order was not much different from the method criminals use. You don't really need me to tell you that—I'm not saying anything new here. Whenever I see a cop in the metro or the street, everything inside me still freezes up. It's an old feeling, and I can't imagine myself without it. I freeze when someone rings my doorbell or when I hear voices in the stairwell. I'm always thinking that they're coming for me.

On that day in 1994 I could have just been left at kindergarten. My mother dropped me there in the morning and then went home to sleep for another few hours. Then she washed the floors, dusted, and cleaned the toilet. She put on brown lipstick and thick Leningrad mascara from a little cardboard box, dusted her eyelids with pearlescent shadow. Before going out, she pulled on her boots and sat down in the kitchen to smoke. The zipper tab on one of the boots had broken, and there were no paper clips or safety pins around, so with the cigarette still in her mouth she found a fork in the cutlery drawer and used a tine to pull up the zipper on the tall leather boot.

She shook out the ashtray and glanced at her watch. The trash man would come at six, giving her enough time to run to the market and the housing admin office. She put on her floor-length shearling coat, her pretty scarf, her new hat. She checked the mailbox, in which she found a notice that a package had come for us from Trudfront. Granddad had sent dried fish, fruit, and sharp southern garlic in a little sack sewn from an old bedsheet. She folded the notice into her wallet and walked out of the building.

It was a frosty December, everything white with snow. Beyond the Angara River and the dark edge of the woods, smoke rose in a gray pillar above the lumber factory. That was my mother's factory, and this was her day off, which she was spending on chores. My mother went about her errands with measured arrogance, and I liked watching her carefully swipe out the grime from the troughs of the baseboards, then wipe the sweat from her forehead with a clean, dry wrist. It was almost New Year's, so on top of the usual groceries she had to buy mandarin oranges, bones for the *holodets*, and meat for the jellied tongue dish. She'd made her list the night before, writing it in thick blue pen on a cardboard flap from a box of red L&M cigarettes.

You already know what happens next. A woman at the market recognized her hat on my mother's head. They went to the police station, where my mother was put in a holding cell—the monkey cage. The fresh-frozen flatfish in her bag began to thaw, and the pungent liquid dripped to the gray floor. At six, the trashman came and emptied the building's trash pails into his bin. My mother missed him, and the cigarette butts in the kitchen pail began to stink. At half past seven, my mother asked the on-duty cop to call the fat cop, an old classmate of my father's. My mother asked whether they had found my father, and the fat cop told her they hadn't, the guys at his garage claimed he'd gone to the village of Nevon, and in Nevon they said he was in Irkutsk. But if Yuriy's not here, who's going to pick up the child from kindergarten? The fat cop asked if there were any relatives who could take me. There are, my mother said, but they don't have a phone, so I can't call them, and they live on the other side of the river. Fine, said the fat cop, let's go get your kid, we can do the search then, too. My mother gathered her bags, took a compact out of her purse, made sure her mascara hadn't smudged, fixed her lipstick. The fat cop ordered the on-duty cop to open the monkey cage. They put my mother in the squad car and drove to pick me up from kindergarten.

This next part sounds like a joke, or the plot of one of those criminal ballads. That's because as soon as he saw an opening, the fat cop started coming on to my mother. Both his leniency and his cruelty were part of his plan to win her heart; either he was trying to settle a score with my father or get even with all the criminals of Ust-Ilimsk. Or maybe he just had a crush on my mother, her husband and milieu notwithstanding. She was a beautiful young woman. But the fat cop had no luck. The trouble is that I also understand the nineties through the narratives of criminal ballads. I'm still captive to that myth, maybe because I know all of Mikhail Krug and Ivan Kuchin's songs by heart. Their cassettes and CDs were in constant rotation in my father's car. As a girl, I lay in the back seat of his cherry-red '99 Lada while he drove around on business, watching the sky through the rear window—the flickering tops of poplars, the long lines of the wires—and singing along when "Man in a Quilted Jacket" began to play, or that other song, the one about the skirt with red pockets. What the songs were about was beyond me, but their simple, happy melodies lit up the world. My father loved those songs, too, and we sang them together. This made him happy, him and all his friends. On the potty I broke out into "Murka," according to my grandmother, my father's mother. Somehow even she found this charming.

No music existed other than these songs, along with Pink Floyd's *The Wall* and Alla Pugacheva's *Don't Hurt Me, Gentlemen*. The world I grew up in was the world of my father's *blatniye* brothers. They carried me around on their shoulders, and I accompanied my father to their wakes and their funerals.

A few color photographs remain. In one of them my father's brothers are lined up in front of the low, sloping Ust-Ilimsk hills. The grass beneath their feet is scorched, so it must be close to autumn. It was something they liked to do, go for picnics by the Ust-Ilimsk Hydroelectric Power Station when the water levels were drawn down because of the summer rains. In another photo, my mother and I are sitting in my father's car. She's in a cream-colored blazer and a bad mood, so she hasn't gotten out. She's exhaling a thin stream of smoke. Her slim hand lies on the seat, and between two fingers bedecked with golden rings smolders a half-smoked cigarette. A gold bracelet glints on her wrist beneath her sleeve. In a third photo, I'm posing against a background of roiling streams plunging down the HPS spillway. My father was a poor photographer, and my small figure, in flared jeans and a tucked-in Adidas sweatshirt, is somewhere at the edge of the frame. The lens took in the misaligned horizon and the cascading water. During drawdowns, an enormous rainbow arched over the power station, and minute particles of moisture floated in the air. I remember the droplets on my face and hair, how the air smelled of slime and smoke.

In the group photo of the men one is missing, because in July he'd been shot dead in the entryway of his apartment building. They shot him from the stairwell, in the dark, and Slava managed to crawl, wounded, to the door of his apartment. The neighbors heard the gunshot, but nobody dared to investigate. Someone called the cops; Slava was already dead when they arrived. He'd crawled up two flights of stairs by the time they got there. He was clutching a set of a keys with a Mercedes-brand key chain.

Mikhail Slavnikov had been a criminal authority. Everyone referred to him reverently as Slava. Under him were the ex-*zeks*, ex-cons, who'd risen in the prison hierarchy, and in the very bottom ranks of these was my father. Stolen goods, bootleg vodka, various drugs, and occasional dollars wound up in our home after illegal business deals and break-ins at fancy apartments, the way dead fish wash up on the shore after a storm. These were crumbs from Slava's table, but my father didn't wish for anything more. He was a marginal figure; he aided thieves and criminals, but he didn't steal or deal in stolen goods himself. In his understanding, this meant he led the life of an honest man, a simple soldier.

Slava was no Sasha Bely from the TV show *Law of the Lawless* (he was probably more like another character, Luka). On the day he was killed he'd turned fifty years old. He spent twenty-seven of those years in prison. Slava's gang was not like the Mafia on the *Gangster Petersburg* show that ran on Russian TV in the aughts; Slava's people honored the thieves' code of law and never collaborated with the police or the city administration.

———

Once, driving us home from the factory where my mother worked, my father stopped the car to pick up a man in a quilted jacket who'd been walking along the highway in the negative-thirty-degrees-Celsius weather. Listening to them talk, I understood that the man had just gotten out of prison and was traveling from the Ust-Kutsk zone, the prison colony, to Irkutsk. Ust-Ilimsk is surrounded by prison colonies, or zones. Bratsk, Ust-Kut, Taishet, and Angarsk have prisons all over. Pull up the website of the Federal Penitentiary Service for Irkutsk Oblast and take a look: zone after zone. They used to be part of the gulag archipelago, and nothing has changed there.

The man in the quilted jacket was, in his own words, just an ordinary *ʒek* headed home to his wife and mother. He turned around and looked at me.

Hello, I said. My mother squeezed my hand tightly. I could feel her unease.

The man in the quilted jacket patted his pockets and found a squashed barberry candy for me. There you go, he said.

Thank you, I told him, accepting the candy. The men returned to their conversation. My father knowledgeably kept up his side, talking about the Ust-Kutsk zone and how everyone there was mean as a dog. How many years did you do, my father asked.

Nine, the man answered.

Ah, my father sighed, that's long.

Long enough, the man said, but not longer than life.

Isn't that the truth, my father said. My mother, upon hearing the length of this man's sentence, squeezed my shoulders harder and pressed me toward the door.

My father didn't ask about the crime this man had committed, because that wasn't done. A person who had served out his sentence was considered sufficiently punished for his crime, whatever it had been. He drove the man to the intercity bus stop and let him know that the next bus to Irkutsk wasn't due for another three hours. There's a bar, my father said, you can warm up there and have a beer. He took a crumpled tenner from his pocket and passed it to the *zek*. The man in the quilted jacket said a modest thanks and accepted the money. From the hamper my grandmother had packed, my father picked out three pies stuffed with potatoes, chicken, and eggs, wrapped them in a hand towel, and gave them to the man. The *zek* shook my father's hand with gratitude and put the pies in his pocket, the same one where he'd found the candy for me. Standing at the bus stop, he lit a cigarette; my father started the car, and we drove home.

My mother was scowling, and my father noticed. What's with the death stare again? he asked.

My mother, fighting back fury, forced out in a low voice that they had a child in the car, and meanwhile he's carting around *zeks* fresh out of prison. And what gets you a nine-year sentence? Armed robbery and murder, she responded, speaking more to herself than to my father. He didn't need her to tell him what the man must have done. It was all there in his face. He could've had a knife, my mother said, and stabbed us all to death, thrown us in the snow and driven your car to the first whores he saw. What wife and mother? The zone's his wife and mother. He's going to raid the first house he sees, live it up, and go right back again. It's a miracle we're alive. People like him don't pity anyone but themselves.

He wouldn't hurt us with a kid here, my father said. And he

wouldn't lay a hand on his own kind anyway. A *ʒek*'s a human being, and here you are working yourself up.

Slava was buried in the best part of the cemetery, near the road. My father always honked his horn when he drove past Slava's section, a greeting and criminal salute. On the outward-facing side of his gravestone, Slavnikov's family had commissioned a life-size portrait, so when we passed, Slava was always stationed grandly by the roadside, watching us go, maybe keeping an eye on the world he'd left behind. I've kept a picture that was taken at his wake; it's in a stack of photos of me as a child, mixed in with shots of my father when he was young, his driver's license, and a church pamphlet of prayers to Nicholas the Wonderworker. In the photo you can see the grave and a table set with a few bottles of vodka, snacks, and seltzer water. Any division between the memorial meal and the grave, lavishly decorated with real flowers, has been erased. One bleeds into the other, and everything on this earth becomes a tribute to the deceased, a sign that he is remembered and revered. Standing on both sides of the black gravestone depicting their fallen leader are six men close to him in rank. They've taken their places without blocking Slava, even leaning a little toward the image carved into the stone. They stand as though posing with a living, respected figure. One man holds his sunglasses in his hand; he's taken them off so that his face, grieving and resolute, will be visible.

I met Slava before he died. My father brought me to one of their get-togethers while my mother was away for a work training session in Bratsk. A few tables had been carried into the yard of my father's garage and placed there in a Π formation; a grill stood nearby on the grass. It was probably someone's birthday. Slava sat at the head of the table for the duration of the party, smoking long, thick cigarettes and loftily waving away the flies trying to land on the skewer of meat on his plastic plate. Music was playing, everyone sat drinking vodka. Slava drank moderately and nodded approvingly when someone addressed him. He was a stringy old man with a long crooked nose. Or, rather, he seemed like an old man to seven-year-old me. He had small brown eyes that didn't smile but only blinked. Something about Slava scared me. The air seemed to grow heavier in his presence. Everything became tainted with power and submission. My father led me up to Slava, who turned, bent down to look at me, and smiled with only his mouth. Are you in school, mam'selle, he asked. No, I'm not, I said. They wouldn't take me last year, they said I was too little. That's all right, Slava said, there's always time for the institution. Everyone chuckled knowingly. He took a slice of sweet cake from the table and gave it to me. I accepted the slice and stepped away. I didn't really want cake, but Slava had given it to me, and I could not disobey. I sat on a bench near the grill and swallowed the cake down dry.

In another photograph, the men dressed in black, my father among them, are more at ease, and there are more of them. They've gathered for the photo in front of the gates of my father's garage. Twenty or so shaved heads stand out against the black. Looking closely, you can see that a few of the men are squatting to fit into the frame, while others crowd behind, some bending down. But if you glance at the photo without focusing your eyes on the image, you can see that all these men make up a single fraternal body. They're all squinting in the bright sunlight, some of them are smiling, in a few minutes the wake will end, and the sober ones, including my father, will drive their drunk brothers home. Eight-year-old me took the photograph; I was handed the camera so that all the members of the gang could be in the shot. There were probably many ruined shots on that roll, and my father, when he had the film developed, must have spent a long time looking over it through the special magnifying device at the Gorizont store. He ordered fifteen copies of each photo to hand out to the men. The photos had been taken on a little Samsung point-and-shoot the color of "champagne foam."

There's a friend of my father's in both pictures. Everyone called him Gray. His hair really had gone gray, and when he smiled, his parted lips revealed the gold crowns on his teeth. He had a whole mouthful of gold. Gray's real name was Sergei, but I called him Uncle Seryozha. Uncle Seryozha carried me around under his arm, produced candy from his pockets, picked me up from kindergarten when my father was busy. He drove a white Toyota Camry with a blue-gray interior. At Slava's wake Uncle Seryozha made me an open-faced sprat sandwich and poured some tarragon soda into a plastic cup. He whispered that I should come find him if I wanted more. As he bent down to speak to me, I smelled a mixture of cologne, cigarettes, and rank male sweat. I studied his porous skin; it had darkened over the course of the summer, and beneath the light stubble beginning to grow on his cheek there was a deep groove. Up close, his hair

turned out not to be so gray after all; he had a lot of grays, but
they hadn't yet taken over. A few dry pine needles were caught
on the shoulder of his starched shirt with yellow embroidery on
its stand collar. Lifting a heavy hand, large golden signet ring on
his middle finger, he patted me on the head. I ate the sandwich
on a bench by a neighboring grave. In the heat, the soda, which
I drank slowly, tasted even sweeter. I wanted regular mineral
water, but even though Uncle Seryozha had told me to ask him, I
felt awkward interrupting the adult conversation around Slava's
grave. Judging by the fact that in the photo from the wake Uncle
Seryozha stands directly to the right of Slava's gravestone, he
must have been the gang's second-in-command. I keep wondering whether he ever killed anyone, sweet Uncle Seryozha. All
the men in that photograph were thieves, murderers, extortion-
ists, rapists. They were brutal people. In the mid-aughts Gray
was killed in prison.

The fates of the other men in the photograph are unknown
to me. But considering what happened to my father, I can as-
sume that they didn't live much longer, or, if they're still around
today, that their real lives remain back there, inside that hot July
afternoon. Sunlight streams through the branches of birches and
pines. The air smells like warm sausage, grease, vodka, wilting
funeral roses. Their black silk shirts, unbuttoned at the chest,
darken with patches of sweat. The murmur of quiet, respectful
conversation blends with the sounds of the forest. Somebody
laughs quietly into his fist, remembering how he first met Slava.
My father brings a white canister from his car; from a black-
and-white striped plastic bag with the silhouette of a woman in
a wide-brimmed hat, he pulls out a clean towel. The men wash

their hands between the graves. A stream of water runs along the ground, sweeping along dry pine needles, birch leaf litter, warm dust.

There was talk that Slava had been offed by his own people. It wasn't just Slava's gang that was falling apart—the entire world was being reconfigured. It was the very end of the nineties, Putin about to come to power. The criminals who'd made their money on illegal logging of the Siberian forests were gradually legitimizing their business. Many of them had established themselves within the city government, which allowed them to go on pillaging lumber in ways that were now entirely legal. However, as is well known, the moral code of thieves, unlike the ethics of the Mafia, does not allow for emergence from the shadows or cooperation with the powers that be. This is why things didn't work out for Slava.

When a dog snatches up a piece of meat, it snorts out dust, droplets of saliva, a small gust of warm air. Time does the same. Time breathed my father out, and he was left stranded in the cold wind of the future. There was no one around now to protect him from the cops, no collective criminal surety; it was every man for himself, and he fled the city.

I'm like the con man who strips the last shred of clothing off the deceived woman's back. Only here I am my own deceiver, my own victim. On the other hand, I'm not actively trying to romanticize those times. There was a beautiful woman with a bag of oranges in a jail cell, and a fat policeman in love with her. A squad car by the kindergarten gates, a crack in the lid of a toilet tank. Slick, untouchable Yura, who made his wife the gift of a stolen hat. A handful of stolen gold he brought her, so she could pick out any pieces she liked. All that's missing is a merry fiddle and Krug's lyrics: *chew the cud yourselves, you copper fucks.* Because my father really did wriggle out of every jam, like a swift freshwater fish. He slipped away, but the music, as the organizing principle of his consciousness, stayed with him.

The mythos of the *blatnoy* song depends on the opposition of *theirs* and *ours.* The mother, the loyal wife, the sidekick—these are the figures within *our* inner circle. *They* are the cops, the forces of evil that the lyric hero must confront in endless battle. Any man or woman can turn out to belong to the forces of darkness, they only have to commit some kind of betrayal—sexual, or moral. And above the fray, or, rather, somewhere peripheral to it all, is the hero's elderly mother, wretchedly observing her son's suffering and awaiting its inevitable outcome: a prison sentence for him and death for herself. The life of a thief or a criminal is cyclical, and every crime is followed by a moment of bliss at some restaurant feast. There's never any attempt to lead a peaceful, lawful existence. The only possible good in the world of criminal song is the ecstasy of a brief stint of freedom, and also dominance over cronies and women. And freedom is sweet precisely because eventual betrayal and arrest are factored into this life, assumed from the very beginning.

There is also another kind of criminal narrative—a tale of remorse and of man's helplessness in the face of society and his own fate. Ivan Kuchin writes songs about this; just listen to his

"Man in a Quilted Jacket" and "Cross-Sealed by Fate." Articles about Kuchin say that he served a twelve-year prison sentence, and that when his mother died, he wasn't furloughed to attend her funeral. This event is crucial for his artistic persona, along with the treachery of the woman he loved, who left him for another, better-established artist when Kuchin had already become a singer of Russian chanson.

In the 2002 miniseries *Law of the Lawless*, Sasha Bely's mother dies of a heart attack during a particularly difficult period for Bely. In a sense, the recent attempt on Bely's life is the cause of his mother's death, though no one in the series says so. The hero wanders through the darkened, empty apartment, addressing his dead mother. His speech is full of remorse; he has come to beg forgiveness for the life he leads. He asks his mother to have pity on him, to imagine that he isn't a criminal but a military man. *They shoot in battle, too*, he says.

The image of the eternally awaiting mother can be traced back to ancient epics. Anticlea, mother of Odysseus, dies before her son returns from the Trojan War. The world we live in is extremely old; everything around us is ancient. The criminal ballad's archetype of the elderly mother borrows something from Anticlea and something from the Mother of God. The mother is the only one who won't pass judgment on her son, who acts as witness to his suffering. In *blatnoy* songs, the mother won't live long enough to see her son again, or, even if she does, they'll soon be parted. The son will be caught again, despite promising his mother to lead an honest life, despite her hope that life can be begun anew.

In such mother-son relationships, the man takes on a dual

role, playing both husband and child. Thus he becomes both his mother's rock and her ruin. Watch *Law of the Lawless* again, and note how it treats this duality within the male character. When they're together, Bely and his friends Phil, Pchela, and Kos horse around like teenagers; they're like sweet kittens in a sunny meadow. They take such joy in their games, their charming high jinks; they pummel one another tenderly, like brothers. But when they're forced to defend themselves, they transform into serious men of action. Bely speaks in aphorisms meant to convey his worldly, masculine wisdom. The boys get out their semi-automatics and go risk their lives for honor. If you listen to the songs on the show, they sound like the soundtrack of a knightly joust. Bely and his brothers are proud warriors. But who were the actual knights if not criminals in shining armor? The only one to really believe in their virtue and valor was the mad Don Quixote.

This duality is disorienting. Bely's wife can't bring herself to divorce him; *I feel sorry for that idiot*, she exclaims. She sees her husband's troubles as a chain of events arising from his difficult, risk-loving personality, not as the result of a choice he made. She considers their life together her just penance, and when Sasha finds himself at a loss, she takes on the identity of Sasha Bely herself, solving the mystery of the attempted murder of her husband and his friends.

The moral system of the *blatniye* has its own interpretation of the biblical verse about the repentance of sinners. This interpretation presumes the right to waste a human life. Lives can be wasted through murder or through the endless waiting demanded of others; they can be wasted through crime. And then, at some particularly poignant, sentimental moment, you can repent—a repentance the people around you are obliged to accept, to take seriously.

My father was sentimental, like all cruel people. Drunk, he'd start bawling, calling me his daughter, going on about my mother being his only wife. In his drunken confessions he was elevated into someone greater than himself. He became more than a private individual; his repentance extended the trajectory of his life into something resembling a general human destiny. I was never touched by his pathos; instead, I felt deeply disconcerted and powerless to discharge the tension of the situation. This was because I was only a mirror, after all, for the distraught lyric hero within my father.

My father went to prison right after I was born. He'd been picking up fares in his Volga and selling them vodka, and at night he helped burglars break into apartments.

You know, for a long time I wondered how boys who grew up as disciplined members of the Young Pioneers became thieves and criminals, until I finally understood that it was a simple progression. They were used to strict hierarchies at school and in the army, and this subordination to the common good did its work on them. Now add to that background a sense of frustration with their poverty and the general bleakness of their lives. The qualities I'm attributing to the *blatniye* didn't come from nowhere. These traits had always been theirs. You'll say that half the country were prisoners and the other half guards. If this is true, how else could the Soviet era end? It could only devolve into brutality. And we are all an extension of that time. This makes me deeply uneasy.

My father never went to prison again, though I grew up aware of my mother's fear that he could be taken away at any moment. Gradually, he stopped having anything to do with the *blatnoy* world, but he never stopped listening to its music. Then again, everybody knows these songs, "Golden Domes," "Brothers, Don't Gun Each Other Down." My father loved them like a deceived woman loves the man who lies to her. It was a love tinged with bitter nostalgia and longing for the past. At the end of the day, these had been the songs of his youth and his brothers.

The *blatnoy* mythos is thoroughly steeped in Russian chauvinism. It always surprised me that precariousness and poverty give rise to feelings of personal exceptionalism, but the connection is really not that hard to understand. People need to find a way to justify their suffering. Over and above the violent struggle for power within a prison colony or a town, criminal mythology always implies war on a global scale, a war between Russians and others. My father despised people from the Caucasus; the internationalist rhetoric of the Soviet Union had done nothing for him. The single circumstance in which he could tolerate a Caucasian was if the two of them had gone through some rough manly scrapes together. He had a friend he'd served with: Gaba, a Buryat from Chita. My father never called Gaba by name, he called him "the Buryat," but he adored him. They'd gone on the quest for moonshine together. Before his service, Gaba was expelled from medical school in Irkutsk. He was a quiet Buddhist, and in his first year he took the anatomy exam several times, but somehow he and the professor never came to an understanding, so he never gave Gaba a passing grade. My father joked that the professor had hated Gaba for his slanted eyes, and both of them laughed at that joke. They laughed a lot together generally, because in addition to vodka my father knew how to find hashish. They smoked together and stared out into the desert.

My father had liked army service; the Mongolian desert resembled the steppe he knew so well. From the army, he brought back a terrifying Buddhist demon mask. The demon had five skulls set into his flaming crown and three ferocious eyes that watched me when I walked down the hallway from my bedroom to the kitchen. The mask hung high on the wall, making it even harder for me to believe that it was harmless. My father sometimes pulled it down and put it on, cackling diabolically from behind it like a villain. Then, back to laughing in his regular voice, he would remove the mask and try to comfort me, telling me it wasn't scary at all, that a mask is just a mask, there's nothing dangerous about it. But if there's nothing dangerous about it, I thought, why does my father turn into a demon when he puts it on?

Do you remember, on *Law of the Lawless*, Sasha Bely's army buddy Fara? Bely arrives at yet another shoot-out, his boys are ready to go, a couple of armed guys are hiding in the bushes. Bely goes to speak with his opponent, and the opponent turns out to be his old army buddy Farkhad. The two embrace and walk down an empty street, kicking a soccer ball back and forth, trailed by ten coffin-black Mercedes. They're brothers—not by blood but in life. What they share trumps ethnic divisions. Once upon a time, Bely and Fara learned to be men together.

When I was a child, my father and his friends called me *mam'selle*: a shortened version, pronounced in the mangled *blatnoy* manner, of the French *mademoiselle*. Strangely, the thieves always had a soft spot for France—maybe because to them it represented elegance and high style, and they wanted to resemble the aristocracy in every possible way, even as they despised it.

He called my mother Madam, like in the lyrics of another Krug song: *Oh Madam, luxury is plain without you / Madam, for you even Paris isn't up to par.*

Whenever that song began to play, he looked at my mother with a particular glint in his eye, and she responded with controlled haughtiness, but in a way that made clear she had taken the compliment. That's why my father called her Madam. Her regal airs and love of luxury were highly prized in my father's circles. My mother wasn't a *slag*, a *whore*, or a *floozy*; she was my father's wife.

In Kuchin's songs, the woman, whether wife or faithful girlfriend, is endowed with a set of particularly noble qualities. She weeps but waits for her man's release from prison; she doesn't cheat, and she will not betray. The price of her loyalty, in Kuchin's lyrics, is the hero's love and patronizing affection. This grown Madam, or Faithful Girlfriend, was once a respectable young woman. *There goes a good girl, at her side a con and a hooligan.* The good girl is inherently a creature of virtue and integrity, and these traits accrue in value as she ages, setting her apart in a world of *street skanks*. But you know, don't you, that there's a very fine line between moral scrupulousness and moral failure?

My mother was a rare beauty, and everybody knew it. She wore little black dresses with tall boots, a short A-line skirt with satin-trimmed pockets, and a near-translucent black lace top. Delicate, glittering gold chains with dangling ruby pendants tangled around her neck. She wore brown or burgundy lipstick. Stacked on top of our VCR lay Cindy Crawford's gymnastics workout tapes. My mother aspired to look like her; in school, kids had teasingly called her a samovar, and she hated her broad-boned frame and size-ten feet.

By the time she turned eighteen, my mother was fed up with life in her parents' house, where perpetually drunk Grandpa Rafik, jealous without reason or cause, beat my grandmother Valentina, his wife. My mother saw everything, and by the time she was fourteen she was pushing back. She sensed that the Soviet world would soon collapse, if not today, then the day after. And so it was, the system was close to collapsing, only in its death throes it went on trying to get under her skirt, and further still, under her skin.

You remember the world-renowned, archetypal Soviet hikers, sitting around a bonfire at night in their coxcomb knitted hats, playing guitar. My mother had been hiking up mountains since she was twelve, and that's how she met my father. He'd come back from the army and gotten a job at a taxi stand, and on weekends he went with the guys to a mountaineering camp to drink vodka by the fire.

I don't think my mother cared much for hiking. Certainly she liked to sit around drinking in nature, but waking up early in a frozen tent and trudging somewhere over snow and rocks, with no possibility of relieving herself somewhere warm—she hated all that. She complained that the conditions on these hikes meant she had to keep holding it in, which finally gave her anteflexion of the uterus. I'm not convinced a full bladder can tilt your uterus. For her, Soviet-era hiking was more of an opportunity to run away from home than a serious hobby.

My father helped her run away from home in a way that was completely legal. I'm not telling you anything new here. How many women see marriage as a ticket out of their parents' house? I couldn't even tell you how many. A lot.

All through her childhood she'd worn hand-me-downs, and now she wanted beautiful clothes, jewelry, respect. My father called her Madam, and this flattered her. Then the system she despised collapsed. What remained was the factory where she made a stable salary—and when money at the factory ran out, she brought home equity. Now she was the legal owner of a tiny portion of her workplace, although those shares were soon sold for cheap. My mother wanted to be free; she wanted her own kitchen furniture, not something communal; she wanted golden necklaces and a pretty black dress. My father's world offered her these things, and so she turned toward it with her wide, beautiful face.

But after giving birth to me, she found herself utterly alone. My father disappeared to the garage at night and drove around on business, and my still-young grandmother, her mother, was busy bringing up my mother's younger sister. My father's mother, who at the time also lived in Ust-Ilimsk, was the manager of a store and didn't have any time for her daughter-in-law or grandchild. When my mother was finally able to drop me off at kindergarten and get herself back in shape after maternity leave, she put on a dress and went to the beer bar where my father's crowd hung out. At the bar she was greeted by the girlfriends of my father's friends, who sat her down and wordlessly pointed out all the women my father had been sleeping with. My mother said that all the hair on her head stood up. My father, coming into the bar, had no reason to expect his wife to be there and simply failed to notice her; he walked over to the neighboring table, where a red-headed young woman was sitting. He bent down and said something into the woman's ear. My mother, who was fond of improvised dramatic scenes, called his name, not loudly but clearly. This would be a funny story if it were in an episode of the TV show *Gorodok*, but it's the story of my parents' lives. To get back at my father, my mother started going out at night, dancing at restaurants in her short skirt.

As for me, I was *mam'selle*. I keep speculating about the fate that nickname had prepared for me, and I stop myself each time, because my entire being still resonates with that insolent word. It's a tricky word, an unclean one. It makes me feel ashamed. The writer Varlam Shalamov writes that "the future of his daughters (should they exist somewhere) seems to the thief to typically contain the career of a prostitute, the companion of some important thief. Generally, there's no moral burden (even one particular to the *blatnoy* code) on his conscience in this regard." Shalamov wrote this in 1959, looking back at the 1930s nascence of the thieves' brutal subculture. This subculture became the place where the ethics of the *blatniye* took hold, sprouted, and sowed their seeds.

When Shalamov was writing, the Bitch Wars between criminal factions in the gulag had ended, and subsequent government amnesties, one after the next, set free hundreds of thousands of the *blatniye*. Nothing comes from nothing, and nothing disappears completely—that's a law of physics and of culture. The *blatniye* who recalled the criminal golden age of the 1930s passed their values and principles down to the generations that came after them. A transformed world always retains the traces of its predecessors, just as a body remembers how to ride a bike and keeps its scars. You shouldn't believe in the new—everything around us is quite old. I keep turning and turning that word over within myself—*mam'selle*—and it resounds in me as shame. It's been around for a long time—long before I existed, it was there.

— 8 —

And I barely remembered anything about Astrakhan. I only remembered the oppressive, sultry heat. I remembered the unbearable feeling that I didn't belong in that place, with my father. When the hot water was shut off in my rented Moscow apartment, I bought plane tickets to Astrakhan and rented a studio in a new-build high-rise near the river. It was the sort of apartment people buy to rent out rather than live in. Every single object inside it was plastic and disposable, even things that weren't supposed to be single use: the too-warm, garishly patterned bedsheets, the stiff polyurethane house slippers, the sewing kit in the wardrobe. I was used to all of it, it was all meant to be cozy and comfortable for me. The owner, as he gave me the keys, admitted that I was only the third guest they'd had. I read the previous guests' reviews in the rental app; they were positive. But as soon as he left, I found a few black hairs on the windowsill and ketchup stains on the shelves. The toilet wasn't particularly clean, either. I assumed that the owners had figured since the apartment was new, any dirt in it would be minor. On the second day I saw more of the same black hair in the bathroom sink, and the air conditioner sprang a leak and stopped working.

I had come to Astrakhan at the end of June, and the city was experiencing a forty-degree heat wave, but feeling no desire to deal again with the owner, or, worse, a repairman, I endured the heat.

The same thing had happened when my wife and I were waiting out the winter in Anapa. On the second day of our visit, one of the two gas burners we were using broke, and for the rest of our time there we cooked using the sole remaining burner. Because of this, breakfast could take up to ninety minutes. I had to brew the coffee, fry some eggs for myself, and make kasha for my wife. Her kasha cooled while my omelet cooked. While the omelet and the kasha were being prepared, my coffee got cold, but after the coffee there was still tea to make. And still, I couldn't force myself to write to the woman who rented us the place. The very thought of having to speak to a stranger threw me into a panic. I was prepared to spend every morning cooking kasha, eggs, and coffee by turns, but not ready to handle a confrontation.

And so now I was living without air-conditioning. What didn't I try instead? I put on cold compresses, soaked my shirt in cold water and wore it wet until it dried. I would work while sitting on the toilet next to a bathtub of cold water, but I would not surrender. I would tell the owner about the broken AC the moment my key hit the bottom of the mailbox, not a second sooner. And what were they going to do, really? When the internet in the Anapa apartment had barely worked, I sent a WhatsApp message to the owner asking her to deduct some amount from the rental fee, and she suggested I just open the door of the wardrobe where the modem was kept. I had no faith in the solicitude of short-term landlords.

———

When you make up your mind to do something, it never works out. I had gone to Astrakhan to look into my father's death. I wanted to visit the morgue and the regional AIDS center, but at the very last minute, when I was already at the airport, I realized I'd forgotten to bring my birth certificate, and nobody would even hear me out without that—you know how things are done here. So what was left for me to do? Instead of the AIDS center and the morgue I went to the Velimir Khlebnikov Museum to read the papers of Khlebnikov's sister Vera, and I traveled into the delta, to the village of Trudfront, where my great-grandfather the fisherman had lived. I took long walks through the city, and I visited my father's grave at the cemetery. Along the way, I made notes about the steppe.

I walked down the street where I'd lived at my father's place ten years ago. I never managed to find the house—a little two-room structure with a concrete addition and plastic windows. A few houses on Chekhov Street looked similar to it, that house with its dark little bedroom where I read books and bitterly masturbated between fragments of early Greek philosophers and *The Story of the Eye*. From that house I had walked into the muggy Astrakhan heat to look out across the Volga. Somewhere around here, my father had parked his dusty truck so he could give Ilona, the woman he lived with, his dirty sheets and work clothes to wash. I passed the liquor store where we'd bought cold draft beer and corn puffs for Ilona's granddaughter. The store's dense air rotated a brown spiral of sticky flypaper, and everything inside was suffused with heat and suffocating torpor. The store's interior smelled like rotten meat, and in the street outside hung a smell of sun-dried urine and warm wood. An agitated branch of acacia fluttered its fingers, casting a blue shadow. Farther down the street stood the church where I'd been baptized. It was the same church where we lit candles for my father's eternal rest. I decided not to go in; the Sunday service had just ended, and elderly men and young mothers with children had gathered by the doors. All these people, chatting among themselves, were eating watery yellow kasha from plastic bowls. One of them started badgering a pregnant woman, nudging her with an empty plastic cup and asking her to share. The woman waved her off, saying that Putin would thank her for her well-wishes. The commotion by the church brought back my old childhood fear. My great-grandfather used to say that if he didn't keep an eye on me, I'd be kidnapped by travelers, pale skinned as I was. They like 'em pale, Granddad had said, and instructed me to stay close whenever we went to the market or waited at a bus stop. He'd loved and protected my skin from the sun; he called me his pale little girl and stroked my back with his dry, blunt-fingered hand. He looked at me with his little light-gray eyes and actually wept with tenderness. The street I was walking down was where, ten or so years ago, my father had rented a house for cheap. The world of that street was endlessly aging, but the people and the plants kept revitalizing and reproducing themselves, the way the fish keep swimming on Vera Khlebnikova's painted panel. Life keeps repeating itself and knows nothing of death.

I hadn't been masturbating for lack of sex back then, I didn't suffer from that, but rather because sex, for me, was more like a panacea. Masturbation lowered my stress levels and short-circuited my boredom. It also exercised my imagination, otherwise starved for variety. The airless days dragged on, one after another. The houses on Chekhov Street alternated: behind the restored wooden cabins stood abandoned merchant mansions; some of the brick houses were only partly occupied, and their uninhabited sections were crumbling and derelict. It was easy to see how quickly places fell apart without people living in them. All these things existed as though in a dream, but I couldn't and didn't want to fall asleep, because I was furiously trying to find the meaning of it all. I could not understand what I was doing there. Why did my father's body exist, why was I privy to his motionless green stare? I asked myself: how did we, people with absolutely nothing to offer each other, come to live together?

My father was also constantly thinking something to himself, and, in the hours between meals and cigarettes he smoked on the front steps beneath a gloomy elm, sleeping. Whereas I couldn't sleep, kept awake by youth and the fear of missing out on something important. So I spent all my time watching lesbian porn on the internet, and when I was no longer excited by the vulvas flickering across my screen, the anuses, the damp fingers with plastic fingernail extensions, I turned to fragments of Greek cosmogonies. I was fascinated by the fact there's an *everything* and it can be fully grasped, in thought or by sight. I was also obsessed with the idea that everything could be reduced to one constituent component. Though, it occurred to me, if you'd never seen an iPhone and got your weather forecast from the entrails of birds, it was easy enough to conclude that people were made of water and fire. On the other hand, though I felt alienated from the world, I could acutely feel my connection to it. I couldn't see how my father's truck, in a straightforwardly practical way, could turn to fire or have formed from water. I also didn't understand how a five-hundred-ruble black thrift shop dress could be formed from air. It had been sewn, if the label was to be believed, at an Italian factory, out of Italian linen. All this fascinated and also frightened me. When I became utterly unnerved by the deep antiquity of the ancient Greeks, my hand found itself in my underwear, and I would frantically begin to masturbate. By the fourth time my body felt as empty as my father's jerrican; I was dumb as an animal racked with hunger and thirst. Having managed my stress, I no longer felt either boredom or disappointment, only sharp pangs of guilt. This was how my father and I lived under the same roof.

Behind my father's grave ripple deep thickets of emerald-colored cattails, and a cuckoo cries out in the willows. The cattails here don't dry out in the sun; they're fed by water from the lowlands. My grandmother tried to save the son she buried here from that water. She paid some teens doing odd jobs at the cemetery to put down gravel and a pair of concrete beams. It's dripping on my son's head, she wailed. She was worried about his poor head, which the anatomic pathologist had split open from ear to ear, to see what he had inside. My grandmother had kept tugging the white-flowered plastic funeral headband worn by the departed over his suture, to hide it, as though the scar were a sign of something perverse. In truth, it was just a confirmation of the worst: her son was dead, and his body, which she once bore inside her own, had been gutted, its organs removed, sorted, and replaced, because all that flesh was no longer living but still had to be put somewhere.

I asked a forensic medical examiner I knew to show me the brain of someone who'd died of meningitis. She sent me a few pictures of a brain as pink as a wilting cinnamon rose bloom. There were several incisions in the fatty pink tissue, and there, in the interior, I saw greenish and yellow abscesses. What had my father felt while his head was rotting from the inside? Trying to understand what someone with viral meningitis might experience, I asked another friend, a journalist, to introduce me to a man she knew who'd quit antiretroviral therapy several times, after which he'd been hospitalized with terrible headaches. I hope he makes it, my friend said. I wanted to talk to him in order to understand what someone experiences when his head is rotting. I was afraid of the encounter and eager for it at the same time, thinking that it would help me gain some insight, to feel my father's pain. But the man died a week later. Meningitis had consumed his brain and tuberculosis his lungs. So it goes, said my friend.

At the cemetery, I saw that a quality black stone had been placed on my father's grave. In the portrait carved into the granite, the cemetery's graphic artist had dressed my father in a light-colored sport coat instead of the track jacket and T-shirt he wore in the almost entirely sun-bleached photo attached to the temporary cross. There's a cemetery superstition against removing those crosses, so they're usually laid on the grave or fixed in the flat concrete slab beneath the stone. Everything at my father's grave had been kept in good order; even the still-decorative fabric daisies had been woven into the fence at precise intervals.

The pink and navy blue flowers were like teasing eyes, stirred by the breeze. All the plastic cemetery flowers were the mocking testament of a hideous eternity. On the day of the funeral, I'd wanted to bring my father real flowers, but my grandmother looked at me disapprovingly. Dead things for the dead, she said, and living for the living. In the end, we bought some unnaturally white plastic chrysanthemums with neon centers. Now they were bound with wire to the low ornamented fence. The wind combed through them, and the top flower was losing its petals, showing bald patches. The cemetery ants, black and fat as ripe mulberries, surrounded me immediately and hurried up my legs and under my shirt. A cloudy plastic bag was being slowly sucked up by the steppe. It had come from somewhere in the direction of the city and kept getting caught on the cross and the spiky, sun-warmed fence palings. A wild blue saltwort bush had risen on the grave, growing out of my father and settling down on the concrete slab. My father had liked to see the grasses growing in the steppe; by fall they all wilted in the sun. Now my father was the steppe, and he nourished it with himself.

— 9 —

The Astrakhan steppe was once the bed of a great sea. It's covered now with the pale and rusty swirls of salt plains, like my father's beige work shirt after a day of hard labor. The salt here feeds prickles and thorns, and tall cattails and velvety silverberry grow in damp hollows. Following old custom, the dead are laid to rest on higher ground. In the past people were buried on the hills and mounds, but now, in places without any natural elevation, they build elevated graveyards. Sand mixed with clay is driven in from the steppe, poured in large piles, leveled—and you get Trusovskoye Cemetery, as the neighborhood containing the numbered cemeteries is called. My father was buried at Trusovskoye Three, the farthest out and the largest. It used to be visible from far away, until solar panels were installed and blocked the steppe in front of it. Who only knows where they're pumping light—maybe down there, into the darkness of the dead.

My father was buried in an elevated mound. Sometimes I imagine him lying there in his dark-violet coffin: the state of his face, what his hands look like now. His fingers used to resemble those holding the frightened swallow in a small sketch by Vera Khlebnikova. They were blunt fingers, like polished boulders; what has death made of them? His grave is easy to find; you enter the cemetery, walk straight until the last crossing, then turn right and follow the concrete path to its end. It makes perfect sense: he drove his entire life, and now his road has ended. But if you look out over the grave, toward Volgograd, you can see the steppe and hear the distant rumbling of tractor trailers moving toward the city. And in that rumbling you can make out lengthy honks. That's the long-distance truckers signaling to their dead. My father lies in the steppe surrounded by the noise of truckers, and on his gravestone, beneath his portrait, there's a large gray truck. When I visited, I moved the plastic wreath aside and looked at the image. It was copied from a photograph I took at the Rybinsk Reservoir. My father had asked me to take a picture of his Brother, and I took several. Then we printed them and gave them to my grandmother to keep. She had provided for this image of the truck on the stone.

When I returned from the cemetery, I took off my black pants and looked at them closely, trying to figure out whether they were good for another wear. The entire back of the pants shone; the fabric was riddled with tiny shards of plastic from a bag that had desiccated in the sun. In the light of the lamp, they glimmered like flakes of muddy mica. The bench by my father's grave was swathed in a black garbage bag. His mother had been trying to keep everything safe from the raging heat, the water, and the sun. I'd always thought of it as simple cleanliness, but now, looking back at my grandmother's habit of washing the floors twice daily and spreading newspapers underfoot by the door, I can see that this looks a lot like obsessive-compulsive disorder. It was the same story with the bench by the grave. There was no other way for her to keep it safe from wind and dust, so she just wrapped it in several layers of a bag intended for construction garbage. Then the bag disintegrated in the heat, and I had sat on it.

I threw the pants in the washing machine and climbed into the bath. My face and hands were throbbing from sun exposure. In the yellow light, my body gleamed white as a piece of soap. I bent down to soap the soles of my feet and noticed a few dark spots of varicose veins on the inside of my left knee.

This encounter with my own body spooked me. I was thirty-two, I had never been pregnant, I had no chronic illnesses, just astigmatism and PMDD. Yet every time I open and close my eyes to blink, I feel that my eyelids are like a clock. Go ahead and blink. A moment has passed and pushed your body forward in time. I can feel time's slow, heavy transport, and my own progress in time is reflected by the changes in my body.

Time washes the life out of me.

Time passes through me like the yellow Bakhtemir River, murky with silt and sand. I can hear its movement and its roar. As an old woman of eighty, the French writer Gabrielle Wittkop wrote that every day is a *tree that falls*. The force of time's motion is equal to the force with which a mighty tree free-falls. The vast crown rustles and creaks as it crashes to the ground. Now inhale, then exhale. Time is heavy, time is a mixture *dense as the soil*. It changed a great sea into the steppe. What else is it capable of?

Wittkop was obsessed with doubles. It's often thought that meeting your double is a message of impending death. That may be true; maybe anyone who has seen their double knows what comes after. I've never met my double, and Wittkop didn't look for hers. Instead, she wrote about them. Her heroine Hippolyte, named after the queen of the Amazons, is Wittkop's double, traveling the world in search of her reflections. Hippolyte goes looking for her own death so that it doesn't catch her unawares. It's a neat trick, and it's what Wittkop did, too: she wrote her double into being, then killed herself.

I meet with my father's doubles everywhere. This isn't superstition or some naive hope that he's still alive. My father is dead; I went to his funeral and was first to drop a handful of steppe sand down on his dark coffin. I have no doubt that he's dead, but still, his doubles are roaming all over the place: stocky men in cheap, light-colored shirts with the top buttons undone. They drive budget cars and carry their keys, money, and cigarettes in their breast pockets. They don't say much. They have bad teeth. People call them working guys, drones.

If you were to ask me who most resembles my father, I'd tell you it's Ivan Shlykov from the movie *Taxi Blues*, not just because my father was also a taxi driver in the late eighties and early nineties, and not because he drove a gray Volga with the little checkered taxi sign on top. Shlykov, according to Russian Wikipedia, is a strong, willful man with Soviet principles. I've thought for a long time about how Soviet principles could coexist with prison time and a life of crime.

There's a black-and-white photo of my father as a child. He's standing by a classroom chalkboard in a garrison cap and holding a little flagpole that culminates in a dangling red satin banner. In another photo, my father is with his grandfather, my Granddad, in Red Square. He's about seven; they've gone up to Moscow to see Grandpa Lenin. Nearly forty years later he took a route to Moscow, left Brother parked at a stop near the ring road, and went to Red Square. He told me that Red Square is the site of Russia's kilometer zero. We found it by the Resurrection Gate. My father stood on the bronze marker and asked me to take a picture. This is the place, he said, from where the kilometrage of every road is counted.

Nothing distinguishes Ivan Shlykov from a regular criminal. He deals in vodka and deficit goods, and he intimidates a woman into helping him find a man he's looking for. He rapes Kristina after she dances ecstatically to jazz. Everyone in Shlykov's orbit submits to his idea of order. He's not committing crimes, he's only using violence to restore justice. His actions seem rational and correct to him, but I believe that he's being steered by something darker. There's no dividing line between "the Soviet man" and "a criminal lifestyle." If there is such a line, then it ran through the mind and body of my father. In reality, each of these concepts justified the other. It's a painful thing to think about. But many things are painful, yet we must think about them if we are to understand why we exist and why we are the way we are.

I'm approaching total maturity. I imagine my body as a barrel of standing water. You know, one of those barrels that stands beneath a gutter to catch the downflow, and you can see the water brimming tautly above its rusty mouth—one more drop and it'll spill over. My body is poised precisely there. I can feel it slowly ripening. Clarified butter, cloying yellow pear—there's something under my skin churning out the heavy odor of a mature female body, pushing it out through my pores.

Once a month I lie down in front of my wife and ask her to examine my chest. My mother died of breast cancer, and I can't miss the moment when a small hard lump forms near my left or right nipple. It may never appear, or it could be developing at this very moment, as I'm telling you this. My wife's fingers are firm and brown; she bends her head over my nipple and palpates my breast. She proceeds like a mushroom hunter or a combat engineer, and I become a place where one can discover anything at all.

I went to Trudfront, saw my Granddad's house. I didn't know how to find the house, so I asked an older woman watering an acacia shrub by the side of the road. She turned to me, adjusting her colorful, belted housecoat, and pointed out Granddad's house— it was one street away from the spot where I was standing. She said she'd known my great-grandfather, her mother came from the same village as he did. She said she knew our whole family and asked who my people were. The Vasyakins, I said.

The woman said, look, one street over there are two tall poplars, left of them used to be the Sokolovs' house, now it's the Grudins', they bought it and they live there.

I asked her whether the Grudins might be selling.

Don't be silly, they live here year-round, they had a gas line put in and an indoor bathroom. If you're looking to buy a house, over there the Savelyevs are selling, same kind of house as the Sokolovs'.

No, I said, I want my Granddad's house.

I did recognize the poplars. They were the ones that cast a shadow over the well where Granddad and I had dug for worms. The poplars in these parts are tall, pyramidal, with whitewashed trunks. In a poem, Khlebnikov compared them to eastern daggers, stuck blade-up into the sand. Later I noticed similar trees near the church. They stood in an even row along the fence, and I studied their long, upstretched crowns. They really did resemble curved, keen blades. The underside of their leaves glittered in the wind like fish scales. This is how poetry works—a precise image becomes indelible from the thing described. Khlebnikov's comparison made the steppe intelligible. With his poplar-daggers he reimagined its scale. The steppe shrank and grew tame.

I had been counting on recognizing Granddad's house by its windows. When he got up, around four in the morning, he would open the shutters, blue with white lacework trim, to let cool morning air into the house. At noon we closed the shutters; Granddad lifted me up, and I pulled them together. He pulled them tighter, and I lowered the latch. Blue and white flakes of oil paint stuck to my palms. The new owners had taken off Granddad's shutters and installed high-tech plastic windows with mosquito screens and blinds. They had painted the fence gray. I peeked behind it and saw that my grandmother's little front garden of oxheart tomatoes had been supplanted by young pears. I could see the old cherry tree, too, the fruit of which I had been ordered to gather from the ground while the adults plucked its berries right off the branches, standing on a stepladder. The injustice of it had enraged me, and I wept with disappointment. The cherry tree had aged, and its gnarled gray trunk peeked through its branches like an old bone. Behind the cherry tree there was nothing but sky. The new owners had cut down my great-grandfather's orchard, the three apple and two apricot trees. Those trees had given us shade in the summer, and at night their fruits fell to the earth, each with the smack of a heel stamping in a nail. I couldn't tell from behind the fence whether Granddad's ramshackle sheds, with his fishing nets and bicycle, had been left standing. Judging by how thoroughly the new owners had redone the garden and the windows, Granddad's sheds must have been long gone.

I've always been fascinated by the fact that nothing comes from nowhere and nothing disappears without a trace. For instance, a crow perched on a garbage bin will always remain a crow. No set of circumstances will turn it into a sparrow or a dog. A crow is a crow, a stone is a stone. A dead crow won't exactly disappear, either. Loosened from flesh and skin, its feathers will scatter through the steppe, ants and worms will devour its insides, and its bones will be borne away on the wind or swallowed up by the earth. The crow will be deconstructed. It'll permeate the sand, nourish the grass, disperse with the worms. But it won't be gone without a trace. The same is true of my grandfather's sheds. What had the new owners done with them? Where had they put the junk Granddad treasured—his old bike, the spools of nylon thread, the besom made of dried rushes that he used to knock down the cobwebs in the corners? The sheds themselves had obviously been used for firewood. The dry old boards would have burned quickly, the nails that had held the sheds together left in the ashes. Where are those nails now? Where are the nine padlocks and the ring of keys, greasy with fuel oil, that opened each one? Say that my grandfather's sheds rose as smoke into the sky and floated away into the steppe. The new mistress of the house used the ashes to fertilize her pumpkin patch and scattered the coals by the fence, where the neighbor's cat does its business. The things of the old world know the art of transformation. Somewhere in the garbage lies my great-grandfather's bicycle. It exists now, at this very moment. Everything exists at once and is never lost.

I knew the sweet smell by the gate. It was the smell of the tree we called an acacia, growing by the roadside next to my great-grandfather's garden gate. Granddad had cared for the tree, watering it and putting up a little wooden fence to keep the village kids away. The tree bloomed from earliest spring to midsummer. Its flowers, pink as tender skin, were always teeming with tiny parasites. It was forbidden to pick the flowers; you were supposed to leave their beauty and aroma for passersby or people resting on a nearby bench to enjoy. After coming to Trudfront, I downloaded an app that identifies plants by their pictures. I collected the photos of grasses and hedges I remembered from childhood into a folder called My Garden. It turned out that a particular humble bush with pink flowers and an overpowering dusty odor had a name—*Tamarix gallica*, French tamarisk. But the locals call it Astrakhan violet. It blooms in little pink branchlets, and from afar its flowers look like transparent, rose-tinged smoke. My grandfather's so-called acacia was actually a specimen of a plant called *Robinia neomexicana*. I drew its heavy blooms toward my face and recognized the smell. It was still flowering. Giving in to the sentimental desire to bring at least something back from my great-grandfather's house, I snapped off a twig, put it inside the book I was carrying, and walked toward the river.

Everything here lives off the riverbank. The ferryman, on a break between crossings, pisses off the side of the barge, right into the water. Two sleek ravens land on a large fish mangled by a boat's motor and tossed onto shore; they shatter its skull with their powerful bony beaks and pluck out the eyes. In an instant, fat green flies are swirling over the birds' heads. They'd been feeding on the rotting milt, but the ravens spooked them. Swift, white-breasted swallows perch purposefully on the mud by the water's edge and snatch up small insects and crayfish. A neat little snake warms itself in the muddy water. Only a young dog, yellow with heat, cannot feed himself, must wait for people to do it. I broke off a piece of my chicken pastry and put it down next to me, and the dog carefully snapped it up.

I made my way down the bank toward the sounds of playing children, and a woman called out to me from the water, saying that I could swim where they were swimming, that the ground dropped away abruptly, but there was one gently sloping spot. It was where the current couldn't lap away the clay in the river bend. I put on my bathing suit and waded into the water. The woman's granddaughters were splashing around with floaties on their arms, floating, and, as people say around there, *tiving* beneath the surface. I sat in the silt-yellow water next to them, and when they got out and the surface of the river grew still, a flock of young fish swam up to my soles and began nibbling at the dead skin on my toes. I was like a hunk of bread to them, one too large to take in in a single glance. They fed on me, and I let them have as much as they could manage.

I asked the woman in the water who she was, what she did for work, whether she'd known my great-grandparents. She replied that she didn't know anybody, that her family lived on the shore and never went into the village, except once in a while for church. I was taken aback by the life she described, but I saw right away that here, by the shore, they had everything they needed—the barge, the water, the fish. I work at the sturgeon factory, she said, and today they let us out early because we sent out the last run of young sturgeon.

I joked that the workers had sent out the sturgeon and the managers had sent out the workers. The woman smiled almost imperceptibly. Then she said again: we usually go swimming after five, after five the water's warm as milk. I brought the girls now because I got out so early.

I asked where else to go swimming near the village, and she said she didn't know, because she just goes swimming here after five, and repeated, as though to herself: they let me out early, so I came here, otherwise we come at five, when the Bakhtemir's warm as milk.

I nodded agreeably and asked her how the sturgeon factory was operating during the pandemic. The woman started telling me about how she had been sick, hadn't slept for three nights, but had no fever or cough, just a sensation of sand in her lungs.

Like someone filled me up with river sand, that's how it felt, she said. I didn't sleep for three days, she said, I lay there on an icon. I lay there asking, help me God, help me, I need to take care of the children. My husband works fly-in in the north, my daughter works in Moscow, I have to live for them. I was so afraid, I lay there for three days with the icon. I was afraid to die.

Breaking from her recitation, the woman looked at me and said as though from somewhere else now, someplace closer to me: if you're wanting to leave, the last minibus for Astrakhan goes at four, but you need to be at the ferry by three. I know because I take that one. I'd show you the schedule, she said, but it's back at home. I take that one sometimes when my husband's gone for work.

Then she got out of the water, put on her shoes, told the girls to come out and put on their shoes, and turned her whole body toward me to say goodbye. I saw a little path trodden through a mountain of garbage. Every day, they walked here through a huge pile of dirty glass and food containers near an abandoned house, so they could bathe in the river. I sat on the shore, my back to the garbage pile and my face to the water, and opened the bag with my lunch.

Now you know that where the steppe is today there once was a great sea, though we walk on the earth here, and breathe the air, as though there never was any such thing. My great-great-grandfather was a resourceful man, a good manager; he built a majestic church in the delta, and people respected him for it. When the Soviets took power, he built a large seafood factory and managed that. While he ran the factory, the icons from the old church were kept hidden. And when it was permitted to display the icons and to pray to them again, they were brought out of hiding. The dark face of the Mother of God and the infant Jesus's brown visage were impossible to make out behind the detailed silver cover that protects icons. It was only later I learned that if you remove the cover, you can see the entire wooden span of the image, the robes and the light. My father's baptism happened at night, in a basin at a neighbor's house, because they couldn't let a child go unbaptized.

A long time ago there was a great sea here, there was a church and a seafood factory, and now there is the steppe. In Trudfront I came across an abandoned house on the shore of the Bakhtemir; it was standing empty, and behind it lay a pile of useless garbage. A long-suffering dog was guarding the garbage and a disintegrating boat. Beneath the boat a slender river snake had sequestered itself, and a tall, tired willow cast its shade down upon them all—house, dog, boat—in the afternoon heat. The house had lost its exterior walls and stood now like a fleshless husk. The interior walls were still standing because the erstwhile owners had covered them with old linoleum. There's no entering that house—the floor would fall through, and it would be the end of you, you'd break both legs and be trapped. All that really remains of the building are the roof and the frame, in which the only thing that hasn't fallen to ruin is a single door. The door sits tightly between the doorjambs. It has a sturdy rusted handle, the kind Granddad also had in his house. The door is kept closed by a padlock hanging from two rusty loops. The people who left this place locked up their house and trusted that the lock would stay. And their padlock hasn't surrendered and won't surrender for a long while yet, not until the wind and the grasses take over the house and change it into the steppe.

There was a great sea here, and now there is the steppe. Let it be steppe, then.

I want to be like a tongue. A tongue is both soft and resilient. When a little wound appears in the mouth, the tongue cannot rest. You know it'll go on agitating it, tasting its metallic tang and feeling the ragged tissues, the sliver of skin hanging off its edge; the tongue will feel these things in order to remember and redress. A tongue is a restless organ, worming its way into the gaps between teeth and running over the chipped bits; it does this automatically, and even when the act is painful and unpleasant, it'll go on working itself into the gaps in the mouth until they are completely gone. You know how a tongue works; I want to be just the same as a tongue. I want to lick at ragged wounds and feel the chipped places in the bone.

— 10 —

Everything I'm telling you here is what I remember, or what I remember my mother telling me. You'll ask how I can be so sure of these things. I've thought through them all so many times, waking up every day with thoughts of my father. I often dream of him, dead: his gray head and closed eyes lying deep in an open grave as I stand above it, looking down into the earth where he rests. Sometimes I dream that he's here, lying very close to me, and I can see his dead hands within reach.

I also have dreams where he's alive. I see him from afar; he's bending over the open hood of the gray, checker-topped Volga. I keep shouting to him, something like, hey, I'm over here! But he's far away at the foot of a mountain, working on his taxi, and he can't hear me. In the dream, my grandmother's voice says: leave Yura alone, let him deal with the car.

What I'm saying to you now are words I've long repeated to myself. It's been seven years since he died, and I think about him constantly, trying to come to terms with and understand his life.

I imagine that I'm doing this because he himself is finished and can be seen as an episode of the concluded past. The only trouble is that I can feel that I'm an enduring, animal extension of my father. I note my walk, the wrinkles forming around my eyes, the silt-water-colored eyes sinking gradually into my skull. My mother said that with time, my father's expressive eyes became sunken. And so my eyes have also begun to recede into my big Tatar skull. Exhausted by the end of the day, I look in the mirror and I see my father's face.

Sometimes I forget that I'm my father's daughter. But whenever I look out over the horizon, at the tops of poplar trees gilded by the setting sun, I immediately remember who I am. When I see the steppe or the poplars, I can hear my father's voice, saying: look at all that space, and we, the *bosyaki*, we run all of it. It was always embarrassing to hear him saying these naive things, that any expanse could be mastered. That's not right, I'd think, watching columns of orange pines flicker past the window of his '99 Lada. It's just not true, I'd think. The forest doesn't belong to us, or the waters of the Ust-Ilimsk Reservoir. We could look at the sun-bleached mounds of the steppe from our car windows. But if I were to walk for a long time into the depths of the steppe, I'd collapse from thirst and exhaustion; in the steppe I was liable to freeze in the winter wind. All that space, which, according to my father, we were meant to easily master, could and wanted to destroy us, as alien human beings.

My father considered everyone in his orbit, including myself and the long-distance truckers, long abandoned by the world, hauling stolen pipe down nighttime highways, *bosyaki*. Before the revolution, *bosyaki* is what people called the odd-job men who spent summers working as loaders and carriers and in the winters panhandled and stole. The writer Aleksandr Kuprin notes that these men made terrible thieves, so the "debutantes," as he calls them, were swiftly sent to jail. The artels of the *bosyaki* were no different from criminal gangs. They were led by the head *bosyak*, who tallied their takings, distributed the earnings, and adjudicated guilty and innocent parties in disputes. A *bosyak* had no home, no family. Their entire way of life consisted of wandering from one night's lodging to another, district to district, town to town. They prized their freedom above all else, and their freedom was their homelessness.

They also had their own idea of justice. Maxim Gorky romanticized the *bosyaki*, which is why my father thought so highly of him. In a literary sketch, he wrote that after spending the night alongside two of them, he found himself missing two shirts. There had been three shirts in his traveling bag, and the *bosyaki* divided their travel companion's belongings among themselves according to their own concept of fairness—each man got a shirt, and the third was left for Gorky. Any kind of work done in order to save more than what they needed was, according to the *bosyaki*, unfreedom, because the main goal of their labor was to feed themselves today and move on tomorrow. For them, being on the road wasn't the means of reaching a destination but the meaning of life. My father felt the same way. Spreading out a travel rug by the cab of his truck and setting down a newspaper, some bread, and a hot plate to warm his tea, my father would say: so now we're here. You know, I keep driving and driving, but I just can't get anywhere.

He didn't want to get anywhere, either. He wanted to drive. Between trips, when his hangover subsided, he would begin to miss being on the road. That's why he'd get into his beige '99 in the morning and drive to the garage and the guys. On the way there he bought melons and watermelons, canned goods, tea and lemonade. Setting out his haul on the table, he'd sit in the faux-leather seat of a KAMAZ truck that served as a bench and light a cigarette. In the shade of an acacia, he'd leisurely crush the flesh of a watermelon and dig glistening seeds out of the slices with the tip of his knife. He'd eat the watermelon and *claptrap*, as he called it, about his affairs. When the bottom of a two-liter bottle filled with the butts of Bond cigarettes, he went to shake it out into the trash. He'd pour water into the makeshift ashtray and pet the garage dogs, ravaged by heat and street life.

The ethics and lifestyle of the *bosyaki* inevitably influenced prison culture and the ideas of the criminals who came later, the *blatniye*. I'm thinking about how ancient this world is, the world in which we live. But what I find most astonishing is how interconnected it is. In telling you all this, I'm beginning to see my father's life more clearly. He was born on August 1, 1967, in Astrakhan. The contractions started in the morning, and my grandmother spent all day walking back and forth to her neighbors' place, in order to use their phone. But the neighbors never came home. And maybe she herself didn't want to go to the hospital. Having wandered a bit around the apartment, she put a basin of warm water on the floor and laid a knife on top of a new waffle towel. After walking out her contractions in the small two-room apartment, she lay down on the floor by the basin and gave birth to him by herself, in the silence of the Astrakhan heat.

He died on September 10, 2014. He was forty-seven years old but he looked like an old man. The steppe winds and sun had gnawed and aged him, HIV had led to the paralysis of part of his face and several fingers on his right hand, and meningitis had destroyed his brain.

Between those two dates ran his long dark life, during which he himself had been part of a larger corpus—the body of the army, the prisons, the truckers. It's a body with a long history, and that history is still being made. That history ran through my father's body and used it to propel itself forward. It didn't start yesterday, or even a hundred years ago, but much earlier, and I keep looking into it, trying to find the beginning. It's a history that's like a cable kept pinned by an anchor to the bottom of a deep, turbid river. Looking at the cable, you can still make out, just beneath the water's surface, the rusty braiding and fraying strands. You can see how tense it is, the force with which it stretches toward its burden. The more restless the water, the more difficult it is to discern. In the darkness below there are a few knots on the cable, little catches pulling at the metal fibers. But there's no way to see them. Bits of dead seaweed, roiling silt, and other river detritus conceal its body from me.

You know, I've always been curious about drowned things. Just imagine everything that must be at the bottom of the Bakhtemir River: sunglasses and watches, money, fishing boats and marine supply. All these things are sitting there in the quiet, pitch-dark mud. All these things have become the landscape of the soft, cool riverbed. The lighter objects slide fluently along, the current pushing them on toward the Caspian Sea, while the larger ones have become habituated by gray crayfish and fat, languorous catfish. All these things, made and unmade by man, have been subsumed by the cloudy riverbed, and it keeps them without any hope of use or employ.

11

Death is easier to accept if you imagine that the deceased didn't die just because, but that he was *taken* underground. The world becomes orderly and logical when you realize that you're losing your hair because your neighbor gave you the evil eye. The world grows rounded and smooth if diseases don't occur for no reason but are rather brought about through the ill intentions of other people. If it weren't for the existence of evil, I sometimes think, we'd live forever, as in paradise.

Some will argue that this is benighted magical thinking, but there's no single way of understanding the world that's better or worse than any other. My mother told me that she saw with her own two eyes how a burning red boil on my infant cheek healed after my grandmother whispered something over it, and I believe her, because there's a bump of slightly thickened flesh on my left cheek. Sometimes I touch it with my finger to make sure it's still there. Over the years the bump has softened a little; when I was a child it was a hard node of tissue. My mother said it was the boil my grandmother had healed.

When everyone had left to go wash at the banya, my great-grandmother Anna, my great-grandfather's wife, beckoned me over and asked whether I believed in God. I told her I did. I was baptized a few days later. A bearded priest sang something and dunked my head into a golden font, then hung a gold-plated aluminum cross around my neck on a lightweight nylon ribbon, the same kind of ribbon my grandfather used to hang dried fish. The knot on the ribbon hadn't been tied properly, so someone had singed it over a flame to keep it from unraveling. The bead of melted nylon scratched irritatingly against my chest. The cross shone in the dark, and I showed it to my great-grandmother. She noticed marks left by my milk teeth and told me in no uncertain terms to stop putting the cross in my mouth.

I was baptized in a crumbling church. There were no icons on its bare walls, and plastic sheets rustled in the windows. The priest asked if my father had been baptized and was told that he had been, secretly, in 1967. The priest took a look at him and ordered him to be baptized as well. During his baptism, my father got a simple cross without any gilding. After leaving the church, we walked down a white street, and I remembered my great-grandmother's promise that once I was baptized I would get my own guardian angels. We walked down the white street, and I squinted at my shadow; I thought that if the angels were to show themselves, they would do so only as shadows on a wall. I kept pulling my cross out from beneath my sundress and waiting for them to appear. I thought that the angels would flock to it like birds to bread. Noticing, my great-grandmother tucked the cross back under.

Since you believe in God, my great-grandmother told me,

I have something to show you. She lit a candle and took a black oilcloth notebook from beneath the tablecloth. There are prayers in here, she said. We used to copy them out at night after work. I saved your great-grandfather's life with these prayers. Women who didn't write out the prayers didn't see their men come home from the war, because they didn't have faith.

I thought of God as the lord of brilliant birds, and everything that belonged to him was golden: his sandals, his apple orchard. God has all the same things we do, I thought, only golden and full of light. God has apples and a fat fish frying on a skillet. God lives in the sky, but he's just a regular person. At night, the white angel-birds visit him and tell him about my life here on earth, about my garden and the fish on our skillet. My great-grandmother Anna was a stern woman who wanted to teach me to talk to God. I listened to her prayers and did not understand how this complicated language could tell God anything.

In the evenings, Grandma Anna put on her glasses and sat down at a low vanity. On the vanity she kept pretty jewelry boxes made of ornate, hand-painted black plastic. The lids of the boxes pulsed with fairy-tale flowers and a galloping fiery steed. The bottom of each jewelry box was lined with red velvet, and Grandma Anna's heavy earrings thumped dully against the lining when she lowered them into the box. She would untie the white cotton kerchief knotted on her forehead and take out the brown plastic comb from the white bun at her nape. Light white hair fell quietly around her shoulders, and she combed it, watching herself in the mirror.

Then she'd take one of the boxes and sit at the table, sliding aside my great-grandfather's newspapers and cups of cold tea. From the box, she lifted a silk pouch in which she kept a few beans of different colors. There was a white bean speckled with brown dots, and another bean that was half black with a narrow white tip, like the head of a pigeon. But there were fewer of these varicolored beans; most were brownish and black, and all of them glistened like the wet beaks of birds. I was strictly forbidden from touching the beans, since they were meant for fortune-telling, but I waited until my great-grandmother left to bring fish pie to the neighbor, Tamara, then went to peek into the drawer of the vanity, where, in addition to the box with beans, there lay a few light-blue hundred-ruble bills. I was given bills from this drawer to buy ice cream and cotton candy. There was also an old deck of cards, warped with hand grease, wrapped in a red rag. The drawer was neatly lined with newspaper and smelled like old dried lacquer.

My great-grandmother would whisper before touching the beans through the silk. Then she'd shake them into her hand and, with her eyes closed, pour them out onto the table. She stared at the beans for a long time before beginning to prod the speckled bean with a single precise finger, moving it back and forth. Finding a place for it, she propped up her head with her right hand and swirled the pointer finger of her left around the interstices between beans. Sometimes she drowsed lightly, sitting over the beans, but upon waking she would begin once more to slide the speckled bean around the table. When she was through with fortune-telling, she raised her dark eyes to me and Grand-dad, told us to pick up the quilted blanket on which we'd been sitting and watching TV, and go to bed. Everyone retired to their rooms, and the house slept.

My mother used to say that if an old woman knew how to *work* something, she was obliged to pass the knowledge down to a younger woman, or her unused gift would torment her after she died. Her own mother, my grandmother Valentina, knew how to cure diseases of the skin, which she learned from her mother, Great-Grandmother Olga. She didn't have a chance to pass on her other abilities, like helping children with night terrors and curing hernias; she had a stroke, and for a long time lay bedridden, unable to speak and curing no one. My great-great-grandmother's cousin Anna had passed her knowledge to Great-Grandma Anna, her grandniece. People said that Great-Grandma Anna had an evil eye and that she was a witch; they said she could spell water to death and a person to illness. They said she could see through walls and read people's thoughts. And people had faith in her and brought her their babies, so that she could whisper over an infected belly button or weak legs. In exchange, people gave her meat and milk. This kind of thing is not done for money.

And so once my grandmother instantaneously healed the infected boil on my cheek. She took the evil eye off me when I was eighteen months old and cried for three days without stopping. My mother said that during her routine rounds the distinct nurse had given me a *bad look*, and after she left I started wailing and couldn't stop. I refused to nurse and would not sleep, transformed into a smarting bundle turning blue with strain. My mother admitted that by the third night she'd been ready to smother me so I'd stop screaming and let her sleep. All those days my grandmother was in the next room, but she didn't go out and didn't speak to my mother, and it was only on the third day that my mother asked her for help. Without saying anything, she walked into the room and picked me up, and I was immediately silent.

The two women actually hated each other, having met for the first time in the two-room Khrushchev-era apartment where my father brought my pregnant mother after their wedding. He had convinced my nineteen-year-old mother not to abort. It's a sin to murder, he'd said. Let's get married. When I turned three, my grandmother returned to Astrakhan, and my father began pining away.

After his death, my grandmother told me my that father had been charmed to love Astrakhan. At the start of the seventies there was a construction boom in Ust-Ilimsk, and my father's father, my grandfather Vyacheslav, went out there to see if he could make some money. He returned a few months later with papers for an apartment in a wooden barracks and a work leave pass. He had leave for precisely one month, enough time to pack up his family and move them from Astrakhan to Siberia. They nailed the windows of their apartment shut from the inside, turned off the water, loaded a yellow Moskvitch sedan with everything they owned, and drove out to build Siberia. But before they left, there was a big farewell party, where, according to my grandmother, my father had the charm put on him. My great-grandparents presided over the table, everyone drinking vodka and red cherry compote. Someone handed my five-year-old father a delicate porcelain cup of water, and he drank from it.

The water was enchanted, and so Yura yearned for Astrakhan like a missing limb. My father loved the steppe; it beckoned him.

My mother thought otherwise. She said that the longing for Astrakhan was my grandmother's own doing, because she loved her son so much that she couldn't stand to see him with any other woman. My mother forbade me to drink water my grandmother had given me or to eat in her house.

When my grandmother returned to Astrakhan, my father became depressed. In the winter, he would come home from work or the garage and lay down to face to the wall. He said that he didn't want to look at this deadly land of exile. It felt like a dark place to him, and the Siberian hills hemmed in his steppe mind. And once he finally went home to Astrakhan, he never did return to Ust-Ilimsk. When we spoke about Siberia he'd grow quiet, thinking something to himself, and then say that the thirty years he spent in Siberia really were an exile.

12

And so we met. Near the train station in Vladimir he bought me a pair of shorts, a camera, and a carton of cigarettes. We walked to the Cathedral of Saint Demetrius and paid for tickets to see inside. The cathedral was dark and empty. Disappointed, my father said that there wasn't even anything to photograph. In the dense white haze, the cathedral looked dim, as did everything else in the summer of 2010. People who remember that summer will know what I'm talking about. I feel bad for the asthmatics and heart sufferers, my father said. They're all gonna croak this summer.

We picked up a large watermelon at the market; my father said we'd eat it on the way to Rybinsk. The watermelon sat in an orange shopping bag, its damp side pressed against the cellophane. I asked when we would be heading out, and my father said he didn't know. Raisa, the dispatcher, was supposed to call him at five tomorrow morning to tell him the address of the depot and the call number of his cargo. He'd explained to her earlier that he was bringing his daughter along and wanted to show her all his routes, so from Rybinsk Raisa was supposed to send him, via

Moscow, to Tambov, and from Tambov directly to Volgograd and Astrakhan.

We caught a cab and drove to the truck stop. At the stop, my father showed me his truck, and I asked where we were going to sleep. Here, he said, and pulled back a little curtain to show me the sleeper section. You're in the bottom bunk, I'm on top.

Why am I on the bottom? I asked.

Because we're leaving at five and you'd fall right out from the jostling, but from the bottom there's nowhere to fall.

In the glove compartment he found a Russian road atlas with old laminated pages swollen from moisture and the touch of oily hands. He opened the atlas to a page depicting the roads of central Russia and showed me our upcoming route. We'll run through about three thousand kilometers, all in all, he said, tracing our path north from Rybinsk with his finger and stopping at Moscow. In Moscow I'll pick up more cargo, he said, and we can also get your return ticket, to leave from Astrakhan.

How long will we be on the road? I asked.

My father said he didn't know, it was up to Raisa. Maybe a week, maybe two, but definitely not more than three.

I glanced at him. He was leaning on the steering wheel and staring into space. The stop was crammed with trucks, so he'd parked his MAZ right up against the KAMAZ truck in front of us. To the left and right of us were red and blue German MANs, next to which my father's Brother looked like a sorry place to spend the night. I felt acutely conscious of my father's poverty, his dysfunction; heavy, cloying shame pressed on me from within; inside this old, busted truck I felt just as pathetic and out of place. My father sat silently, studying the filthy back of the

KAMAZ. His eyelids rose and fell slowly, and there was a light whistling in his nose, crooked from several old breakages. It was hard to breathe in the smog. Gray ash collected in our nostrils, and anything that dripped out dried into a black crust.

I'll have a smoke now, my father said, sleep an hour or so, then we'll go have supper. He felt around in his breast pocket, took out a crumpled pack of cigarettes, smoked out the open window, and tossed the butt onto the asphalt. Over there, past the German trucks, is a bathroom, he said. If you need it. He pulled back the curtain of the sleeper section and lay down in the bottom bunk, and his breath grew calm all at once.

His arbitrary and unpredictable actions frightened me. Over the past ten years he'd become a sullen adult man, and I a young woman. We were nearly strangers to each other. I'd been planning to visit him in Astrakhan, but he ordered me to buy a ticket to Moscow. When I flew in, I couldn't get him on the phone, and when I finally got through, he told me that his route had been canceled and he'd been stuck in Vladimir for a week. Hence I had to meet him in Vladimir. On the last metro train of the night I got to Komsomolskaya Station. When I walked out into Three Stations Square I was dumbfounded by Moscow's dirt and disarray. By the wall of the lobby, a few homeless people lay sleeping side by side, with others sitting literally on top of them and talking loudly. From beneath the dark human heap ran several streams of murky fluid. The sharp smell of urine assailed my nose.

There was a fog shrouding everything; the pavement, the sky, the buildings were all the same color. My father called back and said that I still had time to make the last night train to Vladimir. If I caught it, he'd meet me at the station in the morning. In the train car everyone slept without any bedding, nobody wanted to rent sheets for a ride that was only a few hours long. I sat up all night, looking through the window at the flickering lights and passing trains.

Now my father was asleep, and I was sitting in the passenger seat of his truck. Growing restless, I hopped out and went for a walk around the stop. Drawn blinds in the windows of countless cabins protected sleeping truckers from daylight. A mutt by the guard post spotted me, got up, and ambled slowly in my direction. I stretched out my hand. The dog sniffed my palm, saw that I had nothing to feed it, and returned to its spot. I found cigarettes in my fanny pack and lit one.

I thought about my father. My mother had always said that I was just like him, and I was excited by the prospect of seeing him again. Her words had awakened me to the possibility that my father would understand me. I was sure that when we met something would happen inside me, that I would quietly split open like a ripened fruit and my father would open up to me in return. But he was just asleep in his truck. A languid black fly had been crawling along his shoulder, and in his sleep he anxiously batted it away.

I stood in a lot littered with cigarette butts and plastic cups, the world around me concealed by impermeable gray smog. My throat hurt from smoking; exhaustion weighed on my eyelids. Finishing the cigarette, I threw the butt underfoot and climbed back into the truck. My father was still sleeping. I took a bunched-up pillow in a dingy pillowcase from the upper berth, rested it on a crate between the seats, and fell asleep in a half-seated position.

In the evening we ate at the café by the truck stop entrance. My father ordered *bozbash* stew; he said in a café run by Azeris you should always get *bozbash*. In his deep bowl lay a potato, half a carrot, an onion, and a large chunk of bone-in lamb. Is that it? I asked. Yes, he said. The important thing's the broth. The broth was red and rich with fat, little green dill fronds floating on its surface. My father ate noisily, hissing and sighing, blowing on the potato and clinking his spoon against the bottom of the bowl as he caught the last of the stew. Sweat stood out on his brown forehead with its three long wrinkles. He ate carefully, with the hard-earned satisfaction appropriate to the consumption of a meaty stew. When he finished, he swirled the plastic stirrer in his coffee cup, but the coffee hadn't yet cooled, and he didn't risk drinking it.

Lighting a cigarette, my father turned to me. He looked at me for a long time, his gaze scanning slowly from my hairline to the tip of my chin.

You look like your mother, he said.

And like you, I said. His direct stare made me uncomfortable. I didn't know how I was supposed to respond to him, so I chuckled awkwardly.

What are you doing for work? my father asked.

I said that I worked at a café and spent my mornings making coffee for students and office workers. I pointed at his cup. Not like what you have, a different kind of coffee, with special brewing equipment.

Right, my father said, I've seen those coffee machines a few times in hotels. To be honest, he continued, I don't see the difference.

There's a huge difference, I said. But I didn't want to talk about coffee, so I went on: I also write poems.

Poems? My father tipped his head to the side and pursed his lips. So you're a poet?

Something like that.

So you could write about me and Brother there, and about our drives?

In theory I could, I said.

My father felt his cup: still hot. He lowered both hands to the table. In his right, a cigarette smoldered between two fingers.

It's not that easy, being a poet. He glanced at me with some suspicion. You need to have a special kind of talent, you have to be a bard. He tilted his head again and peered at me from beneath his brows. What do you think, do you have a special talent?

I was completely flustered by the frankness with which he talked to me about poetry. He talked about it as though it were an everyday thing.

I don't know how to answer that question, I said. Talent is a really complex concept.

No, my father said, I think it's pretty simple. It's either there or it's not. Take Maxim Gorky, he was a great writer, bard of the *bosyaki*, the drifters, the poor. If you make up your mind to be a writer, a poet, you have to be like Gorky, nothing less. And then it's easy enough—you're the daughter of a *bosyak*, a long-haul trucker, so you have to write about us.

His loud voice and confident tone had drawn the attention

of people at nearby tables. The truckers and the café staff were watching us.

Do you have any poems with you? he asked. Let's see them, show me what you got.

I felt uneasy but took a sip of coffee from my cup and said that I had videos of some readings on my phone.

Show me? my father asked. I got up, moving my red plastic chair over to sit beside him, pulled my Nokia from my bag, found a video in a folder, and pressed Play. My father listened, hovering over the phone with his good ear. He was no longer sweating from the stew, and he focused on listening, blinking slowly, his mouth hanging slightly ajar. When the video was over, he looked at me slyly, squinting one eye. Now, is that really poetry? he asked.

Yes, it's contemporary poetry, I said.

All right, it's poetry if you say so, he said. Drinking his coffee, he looked at me inquiringly. Do you know the one about the Chukchi poet?

I don't know that one, no.

They asked him, Chukchi, what's the secret of your song? And he said: what I see, I sing. That's you, too. What you see, you sing.

I put my phone away and asked him what you were supposed to sing about, if not what you saw. Pleased with my answer, my father laughed contentedly.

As we walked away from the café umbrellas, my father looked up. It's a shame there's smoke in the way, he said. You can't see the stars. I looked up, too. The smoke flickered, casting a light over everything. My father got down his jerrican of water from the back of the truck, and we washed up and brushed our teeth. Inside the cabin he turned on a yellow lightbulb and unfolded a newspaper. Restless flies circled beneath the ceiling, landing every so often on his forearms and shaved head, and he shook them off with a habitual shrug. I played *Snake* on my phone. At nine Raisa called, and he said we had to go to sleep. Loading's at five tomorrow, he said, and it's fifty kilometers to the depot.

I climbed into my bunk. It was stuffy there, and I didn't have enough room to stretch my legs. My father climbed into the top bunk and fell asleep immediately. Somewhere very close to my left, a motor roared, and the reek of exhaust fumes wafted through the window. A red MAN truck had begun backing up. Its absence opened up the view, and I saw the umbrellas and tables of the truckers' café lit in the distance. The lights at the café didn't go out till morning. One by one, trucks kept coming and going from the stop, their rumbling breaking through my already troubled sleep, while the smog made it hard to breathe.

At some point in the night my father woke, felt around in the pocket of the shirt hanging by his head, and without getting up lit a cigarette.

— 13 —

Morning was dull as dusk because of the omnipresent smoke. My father said that the air would clear when we drove into the steppe. Nothing there to burn, he said. So no smoke there, either.

I had been woken by turbulence and blaring horns. Throughout the stuffy, smoggy night my sleep was troubled and uneven; I kept plummeting into darkness, then being woken abruptly by the loud engines of parking trucks. Before dawn, I was roused by the barking of local strays. I climbed out of my berth and looked through the window. The dogs were gathered at the stop's periphery, sending off a medium-sized Korean truck with a dozen or so white sheep standing in the back. The sheep stank and bleated, and scents and sounds unusual in that part of the country had excited the dogs. A tenacious iridescent fly kept landing on my ankle, each of its legs clinging disgustingly to my skin. The heat had made my entire body clammy with sweat; I kept pulling a sheet over myself, then throwing it off.

My father got up around five, smoked two cigarettes, brushed his teeth, then took out a gas plate, warmed some water, and brewed a large mug of strong tea with a stainless steel strainer.

If it weren't for the mug's handle, I would have thought he was drinking tea from a soup bowl. The inside of his road mug was striped with pale and brownish streaks of hardened plaque left by water and the dyes in his tea. He filled the mug to the brim and waited for the tea to cool, then drank it squinting, sighing and clicking his tongue with pleasure. Clear beads of sweat stood out on his forehead, and the fine hairs at his temples stuck together.

Finishing his tea, my father put everything away in the crate wedged between the passenger and the driver's seats. Before starting the truck, he took his worn Samsung from his breast pocket, checked his messages, and sent a text to Raisa. In the same pocket he discovered an old toothpick and chewed its end to bits; it felt good to sink his teeth into something tough but malleable, something to tickle his gums. He withdrew the softened toothpick from his mouth and inserted it into his nostril. Tickling around in there, he sneezed happily and wiped his face with a road towel. Then he started the engine and steered out of the stop. At the exit he waved to an elderly waiter who sat smoking in a red plastic armchair underneath an umbrella, and pressed down on the horn, bidding farewell and giving thanks to his hosts and neighbors for a week's lodging and a place to spend the night.

My father steered the truck into a large industrial warehouse. Dressed in his spare pants and a pair of canvas work mitts, he pulled the tarp cover off the back of the truck and folded down the side for loading. I'd been ordered to stay inside the cabin, and I could feel the trailer behind me begin to sag with the weight of the pipe. I listened closely to the noise bouncing off the walls of the warehouse, where machinery thrummed and metal clanged heavily. Men's voices broke through the general din, and though it was impossible to make out individual words, their tones were clear enough: they were loading the cargo wrong and not enough of it, slotting the pipes in clumsily and leaving gaps; too little would fit, or lots would be ruined by road turbulence. I smoked, collecting the butts in an empty pack. The roar of the warehouse consumed everything that entered it; there was no way to read or think about anything not directly related to this place. The only thing to do here was exist, that was all. I stared at the blocks of pipes and concrete slabs a few meters away from me, then looked over to the warehouse entrance. In the courtyard, in their proper order, lay more of the same pipes and concrete. Everything here was identical, inflexible, dust covered.

I was bored. Loading took three hours.

We drove through white smoke, and the closer we came to Moscow, the thicker it became. I knew all about forest fires from living in Siberia, but Siberian cities had been built with wind speed and direction in mind, so smoke from the fires and from factory smokestacks never reached the cities. Sometimes, for a few days at a stretch, the air would smell of moldering wood pulp. But that was something completely different.

The roads of central Russia are engulfed in green, you don't need me to tell you that. A soft black canvas unfurls between broadleaf forests and fields. Not an hour goes by without some half-abandoned village clinging on here or there. And along the roadside, benches stand loaded with milk, pickles, fish, and whatever vegetables are in season. Old women selling what they have.

I knew the word *tyulit*, "cling," from back in Siberia. My father sometimes went to Irkutsk for work and used these trips as an opportunity to take me on vacation. We'll stop in Tulyushka—Clingville—for lunch, he'd tell me. Tulyushka is the name of that village, my father said, because it's clinging to the road. I liked eating in the roadside cafés; on the road, they were a rare diversion. Being on the road, as you know, isn't just another span of time. The road has to be accepted and endured. It won't tolerate anxiety or hurry. The road wants to become part of you, to be assimilated and absorbed without any stray thoughts of the place you've left behind or dreams of your destination. The road loves itself, and it turns you into itself, too.

If Tulyushka gets its name from clinging to the roadside, why aren't all the other villages called that, too, I used to wonder, reading the disappearing blue road markers: Pokosnoe, Zima. Between the villages of Siberia lay long stretches of dark taiga. But here, I saw, there was a village at every step. In Siberia I had known every road sign, but here there were so many that I couldn't retain them all. At first I tried to read and remember every place-name, but my memory promptly refused to make room. That's all right, I thought to myself. Let these villages, rivers, and stops flow past me, and I'll just watch. You don't memorize every snowflake you see falling, do you? You just remember snow. I wanted to remember this road the way I remembered snow. And so I stopped reading the signs and let my gaze go soft, sitting back with my feet up on the dashboard. I pulled cigarettes from a pack, one after another. The truck, loaded with pipe, pushed on heavily and loudly.

My father said that we were coming up on Rybinsk and put on a tape of Mikhail Krug's greatest hits. Time ceased to matter; it became like a song that could be rewound again and again and heard from the beginning. This is how time worked for my father, for whom the generally agreed-upon concept of time had no meaning. Krug's restaurant-stage violin had first played in his '99 Lada more than a decade earlier, and it went on playing now. The world was transformed, because Krug's music stopped it from moving on, made it comprehensible. Krug began to sing, and my father roared with joy and bounced in his seat, holding the wheel with both hands. Ah, he yelled to me, all I need is good diesel and some cargo to carry. All I need's the drive.

Right, so we're driving, I said, unsettled by his sudden joy.

We're driving! my father bellowed even more loudly, pounding the horn with all his might. The truck boomed, and he burst out laughing.

We pulled over by a newspaper kiosk so he could pick up some papers, and climbing back into the cabin he asked if I was hungry. I said that I was. Here's some ice cream for now, he said, taking a crumpled, shrink-wrapped cup from his plastic bag. Farther along there'll be villages, we'll get cucumbers and bread, and in Rybinsk we can have supper. There's a way down to the reservoir there, we'll park Brother and camp out for a few nights. Maybe someone will come to visit us.

While I ate the ice cream, he held the steering wheel with one hand and his phone with the other, and kept calling people. He shouted his plan into the phone each time: We just left Vladimir, we're on the Yaroslavl Highway, by night we'll be in Rybinsk, we'll unload there and camp out by the reservoir. Everything would go according to his plan; I had no say in the matter and no right to decide. I asked where we'd spend the night in Rybinsk, and my father told me that we'd sleep on the shore. On the shore there's no need to pay a truck stop fee and there's water, meaning we can fill up our canisters and wash. I hadn't had a shower in three days, and the road, the heat, and the smoke were all making me feel heavy and querulous. I didn't see why we had to bathe in the reservoir, but I wasn't going to insist on any changes to his plan. I didn't know these parts and didn't have the slightest idea about the place where we were going.

I was amazed by my father's nonchalance about seeing me again. He spoke to me as though I were some kid tagging along to help out, or a stranger who was mysteriously dependent on his actions and decisions. From the beginning to the end of our trip, I felt awkward about my father paying for everything I needed with his own money. I'd brought an envelope filled with my holiday pay, and I thought I'd be spending that, but he forbade me to take out my wallet.

He stopped the truck by the road into a village, at a stand selling berries and milk. We climbed down together and chose some fresh pickles that an old man put in a bag for us, a few *piroshki*, and a jar of berries. The sun-warmed pickles heated the plastic bag, and it began to sweat. We ate them as we went; they were young and sweet, sharp with brine. I always get pickles here, my father said, they have good ones, crunchy. We tossed the bitter butts out onto the shoulder. My father playfully aimed one between the horns of a large bull resting peacefully beneath a white willow. He missed and sighed with disappointment. The bull lay there without seeing the tumult of the road.

We unloaded on the outskirts of Rybinsk and drove along the dam, where my father pointed out the locks. Smoke, tinged pink by the setting sun, hung in the air even here, and the world around us appeared smudged, rubbed out. My father parked the truck near the water. We'll post up here, he said. I hopped out and looked around. The shore was empty, treeless, with only scant blades of grass breaking through the yellow mud. There was no wind, and the calm surface of the reservoir reflected the pink sky. Large boulders were covered with pale, slippery slime. I walked into the water up to my ankles and asked my father if the ground gave way anywhere; he told me not to worry, the shore had a gentle slope.

First thing's to wash, he said. He pulled a bottle of Fairy from the crate, along with a bag containing white soap. The soap had dried out and cracked down the middle, like a rotten tooth. In his bag of soap I also spotted a small mirror, shaving foam, and a disposable razor. It'll do for one more shave, my father said expertly, looking the blade over. From beneath the mattresses in the sleeper section he pulled out clean towels for us both, and digging around in another bag he found clean underwear and a fresh shirt.

I picked up my shampoo and washcloth and changed into a bathing suit behind the truck, and we entered the water. Watch how the long-distance guys do it, my father said. First you soap yourself up with Fairy, it's good for getting off the diesel and dirt. He poured some into his palm, scooped up a bit of water, and started soaping his arms, belly, back, and neck. We'd brought along a ladle made from a liter bottle of beer, and I helped him rinse off the suds, grimy with dust and motor oil. He looked at his hands, noticed the ingrained dirt, and soaped them once more with the dishwashing liquid. As for the smell, my father said, you have to go over yourself again with the soap. He showed me how you were supposed to lather yourself, and again I helped him to rinse away the foam. Then he turned to his implements and quickly shaved. I walked off a bit to splash myself with clean water, wash my head and neck, and shave my armpits.

We left the reservoir and sat down on a blanket. The beer we'd bought a few hours earlier was still cool, and we each drank a bottle, alternating with bites of dried fish. My father pulled the bladder from his fish's innards, shook it free of roe, roasted it over his lighter, and ate it. My fish's bladder was stained with bitter milt, so I had to throw it out. After the beer we lay down and looked for a long time at the water. The evening had started out pink and then shed its hue, everything fading, growing indistinct. The quiet shore now lay absolutely silent, a rare seagull crying out as it soared above the reservoir. Silence, my father said. Good. Let's build a fire. I gathered a few sticks of driftwood on the shore; he got out yesterday's Vladimir newspapers. The fire cast a warm light. We roasted a marinated chicken on a grate. My father downed a bottle of vodka and burst into tears. I sat through the crying, feeling embarrassed for him on my own behalf and that of the darkened shore.

Having cried himself out, my father climbed into the cabin

and put on a tape of *blatnoy* music. He turned up the volume as high as it would go and sat with his good ear toward the speakers. I didn't know what I was supposed to do. We were surrounded by my father's time, his world. The night had stolen away the daylight, and now also any peace. I sat on my berth, watching him: he was reclining in the driver's seat in an angry, drunk stupor. Beneath the yellow lamp small flies looped restlessly; from the speakers, crackling at the low notes and squealing at the high, issued the songs of the band Lesopoval. I monitored him, hoping to wait until he was completely asleep to shut off the tape player and go to bed. But he would not go to sleep, and whenever I reached for the dash he opened his eyes and shouted ferociously not to dare turn off the music. I looked him in the face: it was vacant. His mind had become a place that consumed everything and reflected nothing. What did he see there, within himself? He sat listening to music, yelping along to his favorite chords, rejoicing pathetically. His past swirled within him, raging, flaring, blinding him. He was powerless against the malfunctions of his addled brain, worn out by heroin, vodka, hard labor, and the monotony of the road. He was powerless against his dark premonitions and thoughts, now that the vodka had stirred up everything that he normally tried to suppress. What he was feeling now were both the enchantment of his life and its bitter hopelessness.

When I saw that all my attempts were useless, I hopped out of the cabin again and walked along the shore in search of a quiet place to sleep. But the noise from the truck carried, ricocheting off the water's calm slatey surface, and there was nowhere for me to hide from those obnoxious, sentimental songs. And I was worried about my father. Anyone could have climbed into the cabin and done him harm. I returned to the truck to wait for the end of his sullen rager. The beer was warm, and I sipped at it slowly, smoking a Winston. Time passed, a night wind blew in from the reservoir, and it became easier to breathe. The shoreline trembled, though I couldn't hear the water splashing. The music inside the cabin had become the only sound in this place, and it was a sound made terrifying by the despair it conveyed.

I couldn't think, but there was nothing for me to think about. All I felt were a deep disappointment and hurt, and on top of that I was simply scared, because there was no one else with us by the reservoir. There weren't even any trees. The truck was parked on a small plateau and visible from the water and the bypass road. My father and I weren't safe there, but he couldn't see that, since he thought of the road and any open space as his natural habitat. He wasn't afraid of anything here; he'd grown up in the steppe.

Around three it started to get light, and I stepped up into the truck to see how my father was doing. He was sprawled across the crate, arms akimbo, sound asleep. I walked around the trailer and reached the tape player from the passenger's seat. The silence made the space feel empty, and after rinsing my hands and face, I climbed into my berth and shut my eyes. But sleep didn't come; my drunken father had begun snoring loudly and groaning in his sleep. The sun was rising, warming the smoke that had cooled overnight. Here, in the cramped cabin, I felt conscious of my displacement. This world didn't recognize or want anything to do with me. My own father didn't know me and did not seem to know how to acknowledge my existence. I was a companion on the road, a lucky break, since with me around you could get drunk without worrying about anyone stealing the truck. I lay thinking that everything that surrounded my father was speechless and mute in relation to me. It was a dreary, rough, comfortless existence, and it resisted all of my attempts to endow it with meaning. I could think of only one way to describe it—the Romantic way. But there was so much suffering and defeat here that romanticizing it plunged me even deeper into dark thoughts. There wasn't a scrap of joy here, only exhaustion, poverty, and despair. And there was no freedom to be found in that, only an endless sentence of forced labor and brutal, destructive alcoholism.

I looked at my father again. His face was deeply furrowed with wrinkles, though he wasn't even forty-five years old. Thick white slobber had pooled in a corner of his mouth. His sunken eyes, with their short, thick lashes, looked even smaller than usual. On his nose I recognized the crescent-shaped scar I used to touch when I was a child. When he was young, my father had gone diving off a pier and hit a support. Now the scar was hardly visible among the other changes in his face, which looked like the bark of an old tree. I touched his forehead and his nose, touched his cheek, waved a fly away from his chest. He slept, not knowing that I was watching him and touching his face. This man is my father, I thought to myself, but next to him I felt acutely aware of my own orphanhood. We lay inside the old truck's cabin in the smog of the fires burning around the Rybinsk Reservoir and breathed the same air. All was barren around us, and there was no place anywhere for me.

It's high time to say something about Ilona. She knew what my father was like when he drank. He'd get absolutely wasted and demand music, then pull up a stool to the kitchen table and sit there mumbling. He talked to himself in some incomprehensible language, declaring something to himself and agreeing with himself, too. Ilona would leave him in the kitchen and go to bed, and in the morning she'd find him sleeping by the table on a quilt she'd put down the night before. Dozing inevitably on my father's stomach was the skinny cat who was his mumblings' only audience.

Ilona lived with my father out of a rational calculation, the way adult women decide to live with men. He wasn't much bother but a great deal of use. Every month he spent three out of four weeks on the road. Ilona's job was to welcome him when he returned, wash his clothes, get him fed, clip his toe- and fingernails, buzz his soft, already graying hair. They had sex, though it's hard for me to even imagine the possibility. Watching my father lounging by the television and Ilona doing housework, I thought that probably by the time people get close to fifty, they understand their bodies so well, and are so used to living in them, that it's easy for them to have sex out of necessity rather than desire.

That's how they moved in together, too, simply because a man wasn't supposed to be alone, and a woman wasn't, either. My father's garage buddies all had wives and children. What can I say, they were long-haul truckers—people say that they have a wife in every town. I don't know if this was the case in my father's circle, but there was talk about his friend Pasha having a woman in Tambov. And my father himself shuttled between two households for a time—between Astrakhan and Volzhsky, my mother and Ilona. Ilona caught on quickly, because he started coming home clean and fed, went to bed just to sleep, gave her less money, and spent more time on the road and at truck stops. Once she packed up everything he owned—and it wasn't much, three shirts for going out and a few pairs of grubby boxer shorts—and threw the bag into his truck as he was leaving for a cargo pickup. That's how they broke up. According to his old habit, my father didn't take any of the things they'd bought together. He didn't believe that a television or a bed had any value, and he knew that he could make enough to buy new ones whenever he wanted.

How had he and Ilona become a couple in the first place? At a dinner with truckers and their wives, someone asked my father why he was alone. My father said that he wasn't alone, he just lived by himself. His friends laughed and said that Ilona was single, too. She'd been standing with her back to him, washing radishes in the sink. So get with Ilona, the men joked. Ilona turned around and asked my father if he was ready to be with her, and my father said he was. What a bizarre way to live, I thought, just picking up and getting together with an absolute stranger, just so you'd have someone to take care of you and meet your needs. They lived together for five years.

Observing their relationship, I initially had trouble understanding Ilona's tenderness toward my father. Neither could I understand my father's condescension toward Ilona. Khlebnikov, the poet, was proud that Astrakhan was the meeting place of the peoples of Asia and the Caucasus and the Volga Slavs. In reality, it was a place of cruel, casual nationalism. The Kazakhs were disparagingly called *korsaks*. Ilona was Kazakh, and when she and my father weren't getting along, he called her a *korsachka*. She took offense. I saw an ambivalent affection in the way she looked at him, and I couldn't figure out how their relationship functioned. Ilona's love for my father was the love of a hostage. She put his trucking money toward supporting her granddaughter and fixing up her mother's house. She herself barely worked, staying afloat with occasional under-the-table gigs and her son's questionable ventures.

Ilona's son, Artem, had once taken out a small business loan to open an underwear store. When business took off and Artem got his first taste of power, he forced his wife to stop working and stay at home. This early success was followed by a slump, and Artem started beating his wife. The wife resisted pressure from Artem's relatives and managed to have him put in jail. He came back from jail with a little velvet skullcap, bulging muscles, and every intention to go on a walking pilgrimage to the Kaaba directly from Astrakhan. Every four hours, he stopped by my father and Ilona's house to pray and eat. After praying, he'd come out into the yard, where I sat looking at pictures of Bentham's panopticon, and talk to me for a long time about religion and prison life. He told me about how the prisoners had developed a system of communication between cells—the "roadways."

When I was a kid, there were lots of objects around that had been made in prison: a deck of cards, beautifully drawn by hand; an ashtray made of bread molded into something like a rose-bud; even a religious icon depicting the Mother of God holding the baby Jesus in her arms. It surprised me that so many things could be made from bread, and I asked my father how the prison artists got the ashtray to be hard as a rock, or a playing card made from a few sheets of paper to be so sturdy. My father said that the *zeks* chewed the bread for a long time. They had a lot of time in there.

After this conversation I decided not to eat my bread at dinner but instead to bring it back to my room, where I chewed it diligently. Although the bread did turn into something like clay, for fine work it had to be even more malleable, so I put the softened mass back in my mouth and continued to chew. The lump of sour bread became saturated in spit, and I swallowed it out of habit, realizing only in hindsight that it was gone. How had the prison artists managed to chew without swallowing; wasn't bread, and food in general, scarce in jail? What kind of willpower must someone have, I wondered, to be hungry and still keep from swallowing, in order to craft some object out of the bread?

As I was saying, Artem liked telling me about the roadways—ropes strung between cells and floors, which prisoners used to pass one another notes, money, cigarettes, and drugs. Listening to him, I thought about how resourceful people are. Let them be stuck without any personal belongings in an absolute void enclosed by concrete walls, and they'd still find a way to communicate, manage to adapt and adjust things to serve their ideas and aims. People will always find a way to survive. Artem enjoyed our conversations; he liked knowing he'd made an impression on me. But when my father came home from the garage, Artem would get in his car and drive off. My father took his place on the bench and smoked silently, radiating scorn. He didn't like that Artem hadn't bothered to look for a job after he got out, instead going around boasting about his gang ties.

One evening my father sat on the bench wearing a bright-green cotton jersey that was a little big on him. He told me to heat up something for him to eat, but when I looked in the fridge, I discovered that Artem had finished the soup. I called out that there wasn't much soup left and offered to boil potatoes. Potatoes will do, my father said. And there's cash in my pocket, grab it and go get us some beer and sprats. Ilona was away visiting her mother, so we were alone together till morning.

I boiled potatoes, bought beer. We sat down to eat outside and listened to the crickets slowly winding up. My father drank some beer and told me that he didn't love Ilona, but life works in such a way that it's often easier to be with someone you don't love. I didn't know what to say to that and smoked silently, looking away. He didn't have to explain anything to me, I could see it well enough on my own. But he wasn't really talking to me—it was so that he himself could hear it. People often speak to others just to convince themselves of their own rightness, to reassure themselves.

Clocking my indifference to his confession, my father pointed a finger at my notebook computer and asked what I was reading. I said that I was reading *Fragments from Ancient Greek Philosophers*.

What for? my father asked.

I myself didn't really know what for. Maybe to understand how the world works.

You won't understand how the world works if you read philosophers from over two thousand years ago, my father said.

I thought so, too, I said. But maybe reading them will help to understand why we are the way we are today. I started telling him about Parmenides, who thought that the world was a sphere without past or future and that we existed in an eternal present. In a sense, I said, Parmenides's concept of being is a lot like being on the road.

My father hemmed and called Parmenides a crank. He asked if this was what they were teaching me at the Literary Institute, and I said there was more than that.

When are you supposed to be writing books if you're spending all your time reading philosophy? Have you written much while you've been studying there?

A couple of poems, I said, but I don't really like them.

What about there, what do you have there, my father asked, pointing at my black-and-white Kindle.

Discipline and Punish, by Michel Foucault, I said.

Foucault's not a Greek, my father said.

No, he's a twentieth-century French philosopher. He was interested in why we live the way we do and think the way we think. This is a book about the principles underlying prisons. I described the idea of the panopticon, and my father, who had been listening intently, said that the only people who understand prison are the ones who've been there.

Do you understand prison? I asked him.

I was in a long time ago, it's different now, my father said.

But the principle is still the same, I said.

Taking a swallow of his beer, my father replied that only thieves had principles, while prisons were built by bitches and dumb cops, who have no principles at all.

In the second half of the *Odyssey*, Odysseus returns to Ithaca disguised as a wandering beggar. He reveals his true identity to his son, and together the two of them methodically plan the murder of Penelope's suitors. Then Odysseus speaks with his wife and requests that the oldest woman among the servants wash his feet. The ancient wet nurse notices the resemblance this bedraggled stranger bears to her king; she can't fail to recognize the familiar body, the well-known voice. Odysseus lowers a leg into the washbasin, and on his knee she sees the scar he acquired while hunting wild boar on his grandfather's lands. Homer tells the story of the boar hunt in great detail before turning all this into a comic scene in which the old nurse is so surprised she knocks over the basin and has to refill it to finish attending to Odysseus. Poets have invented many strategies to maintain tension, command attention, and *impress*. Literary criticism calls this anticlimax, or narrative retardation. I have no desire to impress you, but I do want you to be interested. And yet there was nothing interesting about my father's relationship with Ilona. He gave her HIV, and they kept the transmission secret. Both of them considered death inevitable and believed there was no way to delay it. I've already told you that she loved him like a hostage. And so she was his hostage; her tenderness and devotion to him were the tenderness and devotion of a doomed woman. She flitted in circles around him like a fitful butterfly. She was trying to spin at least something out of this fatal union.

— 15 —

I can still smell the Rybinsk Reservoir. Everything at the reservoir was dimmed by the smoke, which mingled with the smell of stagnant bog water. It hadn't rained for a long time, and the shallow reservoir was blooming with algae. We dipped into it for water to rinse our dishes and our vegetables, and my father drew its water to clean the cabin rugs and fill up his jerrican. In the three days we spent parked there, none of his trucker friends showed up, and my father fell into a gloom by himself.

He called them but refused to tell them anything—though there wasn't anything to tell, these were pointless calls, just to assuage his anxiety. But you know, don't you, that anxiety can't be managed with phone calls, that anxiety is always there within you? For my father, calming his anxiety even a little meant driving. But we were camped by the water, which depressed him. On the second day, waking from his vodka blackout, he climbed into the cabin, drew the curtains, and turned on a little black TV. The rickety steel antenna could barely pick up a signal; fuzzy white lines ran across the screen, and the voices of the anchormen were almost inaudible. But the interference didn't bother or annoy my father, and he was still watching the news when I peered into the cabin. I asked if he could make anything out among the noise and static, and he said, lazily: a little, you can make out a little bit anyway.

He isn't bothered by the white noise, I thought to myself, because it creates a sense of continuous motion and the conquest of distance. Eking out bits of meaning, my father was accomplishing something very similar to the work he did driving cargo from place to place. My father said he only needed the TV for long stops. When you're driving, he said, you don't need the box. I have my own kind of 3D, he said, pointing at his windshield and the windows on either side.

In that case you're driving inside a television, I said.

Well, that depends on how you look at it, my father said, laughing. When I'm driving, he continued, everything flows around me, and I'm happy with that.

I had been anticipating seeing my father again, but for him my presence was nothing out of the ordinary. He slotted me immediately into his life on the road. I was supposed to tidy up the sleeper section of the cabin and the crate where he kept his mug, pack of tea, and round metal candy tin of instant coffee. I changed the newspaper that lined the bottom of the crate, shaking out tea dust and bits of sticky sugar. Mixing sand with cleaning solution, I scrubbed at the stains on his mug—it turned out to be bright red on the inside. I rubbed away the grease on his forks, knives, and spoons and wrapped them in a clean towel. Bending toward the crate, I accidentally kicked the orange bag with the watermelon we had bought back in Vladimir. To my father, busy washing the rugs, I shouted that we'd forgotten about the watermelon. He asked if it had any cracks or soft dents. I rolled the watermelon out from beneath the seat and examined it: it was still intact. When we head toward Moscow we'll pick up some bread and have them together, my father called over to me loudly.

We climbed into the cabin. My father was pleased by the upcoming drive; he turned on the radio, and we pulled out. Toward the end of the country road, before the highway, he stopped the truck by a little red-painted store and bought a loaf of sour village bread. When we're leaving Rybinsk we can stop and eat this with the watermelon, he said. Over there, he added, motioning toward the reservoir, there's the Mother Volga monument, but we can't drive to it in a truck. You have internet, pull up what it looks like, it's beautiful.

I googled the name of the monument and stared at it on my Nokia. Yes, very pretty, I agreed.

Internet's not the same, though, my father said. You have to see it in real life.

Before Moscow we had to clean the trailer. We turned off the paved road onto a country lane, steering the truck into a pocket lined with plastic garbage caught in the grass, then drove deeper, into the thickets. My father backed up the truck beneath some bushes and changed into filthy work clothes. His canvas work pants were missing all their buttons, and even the zipper was broken; he kept them up with a rope. He pulled on a dusty acrylic hat. I asked why he needed a hat in the heat. So I don't have to wash later, he said. From the depths of the trailer he brought out a broom and ordered me to fetch the water canister. I climbed into the back with him and poured the water on the wood-plank floor, and he began to sweep. The little wood chips and planks that jiggled loose I gathered and threw out beneath the willows. My father, meanwhile, swept and sang, just for the hell of it, no particular song and no melody. He sang his own tune, and it cheered him and broke through the hush of the quiet world. I helped him finish cleaning the trailer and then wash the dust from his hands, torso, and neck.

Now, my father said, we can eat the watermelon. He lifted it out of the truck, put it on the side step, and sliced it up still inside its bag. I took out the loaf of bread and broke it open. He had taught me to eat watermelon and bread back when I was a kid—you're supposed to take the pink flesh and the bread into your mouth in equal proportion and chew it all very thoroughly. The bread tasted sour and tacky, and the watermelon crunched and soaked the crumb with its juice. My father, slicing into it, said with satisfaction that we got a sweet red one. He passed the first slice to me, and I bit into it. The cool, sugary juice streamed down my chin and neck, ran from my fingers to my elbow. My father liked that the watermelon juice ran and grew sticky; he liked the loud snap of the rind as he broke a slice off all the way. After finishing his first piece, he took aim and sent the rind flying into the trees. A fly landed in the pink juice that had pooled at our feet; quick little ants came crawling. It's good bread, too, my father said, topping a piece of crust he'd torn from the loaf with a slice of watermelon.

He opened his mouth wider and bit into his open-faced sandwich. Everything we were doing made him happy, and he asked me to take a picture of us eating the watermelon. I passed the camera to him, and he snapped a picture of me with the largest slice. I suggested that we take a selfie and stretched the camera in front of us, dipping my head toward my father's and pressing the button. He was pleased that the two of us could fit into a single shot. I took another photo like that while he was driving. For the picture, he put on his reflective sunglasses and folded his arms on his knees, across his brown stomach. His whole being exuded importance.

The sounds of our voices had summoned some stray dogs. They stopped at a distance to wait for us to leave, so they could finish whatever we left behind. But we had nothing to leave for them. We'd polished off the last can of stewed meat the day before, using the remains of our bread to soak up the contents, and in the morning we'd made strong coffee with condensed milk, which I drank while finishing the dried fish. The taste of the sweet, hot coffee was even more intense that way, and my tongue burned with salt that had collected in the groove along the fish's back. After a breakfast of fish and coffee, my father said that we really had to have lunch at a café. We can get an omelet there, and *bozbash* and some vegetable salad with mayo. I couldn't wait until lunch; hunger was making my body feel weightless and at the same time ungainly and bloated. The watermelon only relaxed me, and when we got back on the road I fell asleep immediately, leaning on the crate.

Nearer to Moscow the smoke was thicker. My father said that while I was sleeping, his friend Fyodor had called to report that there was so much smoke in Moscow you couldn't see your own hands. Look, there's a café over there, he said. By the side of the road stood some colorful structures with corrugated metal siding, each crowned by a sign bearing a name like Svetlana or Motor. Some of the signs were hand painted, others had LED lights flickering even during the day. There were announcements pasted up at every café, too: go here to buy vegetables and fish, here to spend the night, here to hire a tow truck. Sedans and trucks were parked in a line by the curb.

That's where we're headed, said my father, pointing at the plainest structure. They have good *pelmeni*.

What about the *bozbash*? I asked.

It's another hundred kilometers to the *bozbash*, and I'm hungry and need a rest, my father said. We walked into the stuffy pavilion.

There was no one at the tall bar counter, but at every table, each one covered with a gaudy oilcloth, sat a couple of men. My father nodded to one of them, who placidly returned the greeting, inviting us to take his table. I'm getting on the road, he said.

Where to? my father asked.

Driving Moscow to Rybinsk, the man told us. He rose from the table, and I saw the enormous round belly straining against his orange mesh shirt. His face shone with grease, and on his forearm was a dark-blue army tattoo.

We're just coming from there, my father said. How's Moscow, still standing?

It's standing, said the man. He shrugged and left. Our arrival hadn't distracted the other drivers from their meals or from the television, on which they were watching soccer. We approached the counter, and right away the wood-bead curtain separating the kitchen from the bar began to quiver and click. A little woman in a spattered blue apron emerged, and my father flipped over the sticky laminated menu and pointed at the mutton *pelmeni* dumplings, two orders. Also shortbread, 3-in-1 coffee, and tomato salad with red onion. The waitress asked us to wait and eventually brought out the salad, coffee, and cake on a red plastic tray. She'd written down our order in a little spiral notepad and added up the check on gray copy paper. My father asked her to wait in case we ordered something else. You can pay again when you do, the woman said crisply, and rapped a fingernail against the keys of her calculator. All right, my father said, and sat down at the table that had been left to us.

Fifteen minutes later the *pelmeni* were ready, and the waitress brought us two deep ceramic bowls. My father's had a blue design around the rim, mine had a sunflower. All the tables were supplied with red bottles of cheap ketchup and vinegar, but we were served mayonnaise in a separate crystal ramekin. A pat of yellow butter was melting over the hot gray dough of the *pelmeni*. I speared one with my fork and bit into it: the meat inside was sweet and gave off a smell of tail fat. In the corner by the counter a tall refrigerator stood crackling quietly, dark because the bulb lighting the bottles had burned out. I made out some lemonade inside.

Let's get a few bottles of Duchess for the road? I asked. My father nodded in affirmation and without looking pulled out and passed me a violet five-hundred-ruble bill. Get yourself some beer, too, he said. Mixed together on the bottom shelf of the fridge there were bottles of Carlsberg, Tuborg, and Zhigulevskoye. I helped myself to two bottles of Zhigulevskoye and a couple of Duchess sodas.

My father's question about Moscow had a dual meaning. First, it implied that Moscow hadn't gone anywhere but continued to stand there, sucking the blood of honest working folk, and, like a black hole, swallowing all the money and objects that were silently and blindly traveling toward it, over land, sea, air, and wire. (Moscow, my father once said, will eat you up before you can bat an eye. All it wants is your will and your wallet. And if your wallet's empty and you don't know how to fill it, too bad for you. Moscow will swallow you, and you'll go down easy. It's a horrible place, I hate it.)

The second meaning of his question had to do with the fact that Moscow roads were constantly congested. Sometimes, my father said, you get onto the MKAD, the Moscow Automobile Ring Road, in the morning, and you can't get off till evening. And now they're not even letting large vehicles into the city at all during the day, so loading or unloading within city limits has to happen in the middle of the night. This drove my father mad. Anything that had to do with Moscow made him angry. He thought of it of as a vast hellhole, the greatest evil in the life of a long-distance trucker. He looked down condescendingly on the city and everyone who moved there to find work. My father genuinely could not understand why anyone would choose to live in Moscow when there was so much space everywhere else. He used to say that Moscow was a goddamn anthill, he felt so cramped and bored there. People and houses all over, he would say. These things cut him off from space.

16

A year later he accepted a route to Moscow so he could visit me at the Lit Institute dorm. It was a golden, sparkling September, and my father called me from a stop in the south of the city, near the Kashirskaya metro station. I waited there for him for a long time, sitting on a bench in the public square and drinking warm draft kvass out of a plastic cup. He showed up after an hour and a half, offering no explanation for his lateness, since in general he never felt the need to explain anything, but from his appearance I could tell that he'd gone to take a shower. After the long wait I needed a restroom, and we found a blue public toilet and paid ten rubles to the old woman sitting in the booth. I passed my backpack to my father to hold. The smell was nauseating, but I had no choice; walking out, I felt that in the minute I'd spent inside, I too had picked up this unbearable odor. I felt suffocated by myself.

My father stood smoking by a strip of grass. He was dressed in his city clothes: Ilona had put together an outfit for him, and he'd changed into it after showering at the truck stop. He wore a clean, short-sleeved shirt, ironed back in Astrakhan, with a zipper, which according to old habit he hadn't zipped up all the way. The wide sleeves of the shirt stuck out sharply, and somehow it sat on my father like a costume on a paper doll. His gray cotton slacks fell onto stiff, square-nosed shoes. He was holding a plastic bag that gave off a smell of dried fish; inside, next to a string of gray fish, lay a pair of striped pink socks. That's for you, from Ilona, my father said. Tell her thank you for me, I said, sliding the bright bag into my backpack.

My father said that we would now catch a cab and head to the vegetable depot. They sell watermelons, tomatoes, grapes, right out of the trucks. I couldn't see why we needed to go to the depot, so I asked him.

What do you mean why, he said. So we can get you stocked.

But I have everything I need, I said, flustered.

So you'll have a little more, my father replied.

We walked out to the road, my father held out his arm, and a beige Niva stopped for us (he let foreign cars go by on principle). My father explained to the driver where we wanted to go and looked up at me, asking for the address of my dormitory. It's on Dobrolyubov Street, I told him. My father dove into the Niva again, and a moment later was peering out from inside, beckoning me over. Get in, he called, let's go get you stocked up.

The cabbie drove us for a long time through sleeper neighborhoods of high-rises and then into the industrial zone. My father, sitting in the front, had started chatting with him right away: they talked about the price of diesel and rumors of road reforms, and my father complained indignantly about the terrible roads of Volgograd Oblast, not neglecting to add that he also hated Moscow. This was his usual mode of conversation. I was used to the fact that he didn't know how to talk to me and when another man was around would speak only to him.

It was like that when I was a kid, too, and my father brought me along to his garage. The men sat around a table smoking and tapping their ash into a can. An entire wall of their trailer was covered in posters of naked women. The men chatted among themselves, arguing and laughing, and against this background of tanned beauties, their oil-stained denim jackets, sweaters, and unshaven faces looked coarse. Sitting by the garage entrance on a log stained with engine oil, I played with a plastic kangaroo from a Kinder Surprise egg, and peeked occasionally into the dim trailer, where the men were discussing car repairs and the price of parts; forgetting about me entirely, they would start swearing and gesturing furiously. This isle of men in darkness was lit by a fluorescent lamp, and as things got heated they began to resemble a flock of angry geese. I was given a gingerbread cookie from their drivers' table, though I didn't like gingerbread. It made my fingers sticky, and the dry dough tasted overly sweet and stale. I gnawed the cookie slowly, then went to the water pump to wash my hands.

Whenever one of the men remembered my existence, he shushed the rest and told them to quit cursing. But eventually they would forget all over again that I was there, and their voices would rise, the conversation deteriorating into a rough-and-tumble quarrel. When I got bored of playing by the garage, I climbed into the back of my father's car and lay staring at the patterns of condensation on the glass and at my own palms. The back seat smelled like rubber, tobacco, and fuel, and I brought my face close to the upholstery and watched as the resultant optical illusion dissolved the diamond pattern of the fabric.

At the garage and at truck stops, I was left to my own devices and could wander the lot, picking dandelions and scratching dirty dogs. But in a car, space is limited; there's nowhere to run. Everything became subordinate to my father's conversation with this other man, and my exclusion from that conversation felt stifling. I leaned my forehead against the glass and watched gray concrete factories with large signs alternate with scuffed automatic gates. The cabbie braked before an enormous brown puddle, carefully steered the Niva into it, and, skidding, rolled out onto the pavement.

Over here, my father said, pull over. In the course of their conversation he had befriended this man; he knew how to talk to everyone like an old pal of his. It may have been the old habit of a cab driver, but more likely it was something particular to him, which had made his life as a driver easier. He and the driver of the Niva agreed to pick out fruit and vegetables at the market together. My father would pay for everything, and this would go toward the cost of our ride.

The cabbie steered the Niva slowly down the rutted road between warehouses and auto shops. Turn into there, my father said—the cabbie hung a right, and the market path opened up before us. Mountains of fruits and vegetables illuminated the space. There was a smell of warm dirt and fermented apples. Black crows screeched from the tops of trucks, and their cawing merged with the general din of engines, exhortations, and squabbling. Trucks honked periodically, and market workers walked down the rows pushing low, wheeled metal platforms—they were transporting mounds of grapes, eggplant, and pork. Spotting a pile of pinkish-gray hogs, my father asked whether my dorm room had a fridge.

I said there wasn't one. Too bad, my father said, or we'd get you some meat for a mince. We fell in with the crowd of workers, peddlers, occasional women with cloth carts, and wholesale buyers, passing as a trio between the backs of vegetable trucks that served as display cases and storage rooms at once.

They don't sell by the kilo here, my father said, you have to buy by the case. We were making our way through the crowds on the central path, and I noticed that after every ten trucks a new row branched off from the main walkway. Wandering alongside the shoppers were skinny, dirty stray dogs sniffing at bags, and though the fruit and vegetable peddlers chased them off whenever they spotted them, the dogs obediently trotted a few meters away, then slowed down again to continue their quest.

My father said all the food here was basically the same, because the fruits and vegetables were brought in from the same fields. The only difference was in the price. So I should just point at what I wanted, and he would handle the haggling. But I didn't want anything. My father felt that he had to take care of me, and his care consisted in feeding me. We were standing in the middle of the market in a morass of dirt and rotting fruit, and I was supposed to pick out several cases of food. I pointed toward some green grapes, completely at random. No, my father said, those have seeds, that's no good. He asked the seller if he had any seedless sultana grapes, and the guy hopped up into the back of the truck and emerged with a case of small grapes.

How much? my father asked.

I'll do it for seven hundred, said the seller.

I don't think so, brother, that sounds a little high, my father said, looking at him suspiciously.

The seller, his face set in an imperturbable expression, replied that seven hundred was a good price, average for the market.

The hell with you, my father said quietly, and turned away. He took me by the elbow and walked us deeper into the market. We'll see what they have there, at the end of the row, it's always cheaper at the ends, he said. And so it was—a case of seedless grapes at the end of the row cost five hundred rubles. We decided to stop looking and bought three cases of different kinds of grapes, a case of tomatoes, and two big sacks of nectarines.

The Niva driver finished picking out his vegetables, and my father stopped a worker pushing an empty cart and gave him two hundred-ruble bills to get our haul to the car. We loaded our purchases onto the metal cart, and the worker began wheeling it toward the exit, my father, acting as helmsman, giving him directions. Passing the greedy peddler, my father called out to him and motioned toward our grapes. Fiver! he shouted. The man shrugged and turned away from us. On the way out, my father managed to talk a wholesaler into selling us ten watermelons and three melons. The wholesaler didn't take long to consider, just took a thousand for the lot and loaded the fruit onto our cart.

Why do you need so many? I asked.

What do you mean why? my father said. For your dorm and for my truck stop, to treat the guys.

In my room at the dorm my father perched on my bed and looked around. Not bad, he said. How many of you live in here?

Three of us, I said, gesturing toward the bunk bed.

Even better, my father said. Good to have company, and the

grapes will get eaten. He asked for the bathroom, and I walked him down the yellow corridor. After leaving the stall, my father, pleased that I was living in Moscow practically for free, suggested we go into the city center. We took a trolleybus to Tsvetnoy Boulevard, then walked to the Pushkinskaya stop, since he wanted to see the Literary Institute. I showed him the statue of Alexander Herzen in the courtyard and took him through the halls of the main building. It used to look very different, I explained, pointing out walls that had been built in place of an arcade. My father took this in. Indoor spaces made him feel stifled and bored. Let's go drink some beer, he said.

At the Crimson Sails supermarket on Bolshaya Bronnaya Street we bought four bottles of Zhigulevskoye beer, then took Bogoslovsky Lane to Tverskoy Boulevard and sat down on a bench. My father found a lighter in his breast pocket and opened the bottles. The beer was warm and had been shaken up by our walk, but I managed to suck up the foam that flowed from the bottle.

It was a warm, transparent evening. We drank silently and smoked. There wasn't anything for us talk about. My father was proud that I had gotten a scholarship spot at the Gorky Literary Institute, and he said so several times, without cause or context. It's good that you'll have a higher education, I never even got a tech diploma. You need a license to drive, not a degree. Now, your mother, she got a vocational degree so she could work at the factory. Maybe you'll become someone important, he continued. A great Russian writer, like Gorky or Tolstoy.

I was unnerved by this conversation.

To be a writer, my father went on, you need a particular kind of wisdom, writerly wisdom. A writer has to be able to love and pity anyone.

But to begin with, I said to him, writers have to understand themselves.

That may be true, my father said. But the main thing is pity and love for others.

I listened to him without seeing how he could so easily believe that I would become a writer. I didn't particularly believe it myself. I thought that in this life you just had to be able to hang on, even if only until the next day. Whereas to be a writer, I thought, you had to know a lot ahead of time, and to feel certain that you belonged in this world. I did not feel that I belonged. I felt that in Moscow the two of us, my father and I, were foreign elements, people nobody needed. We were superfluous even to each other and ourselves.

I glanced over at him: he sat leaning on his widespread legs, holding a beer in one hand and a cigarette in the other. Over the course of the day in Moscow his ironed shirt had begun to droop, his shoes were covered with dust. Evening was coming on, the kind of evening that swells for a long time with the setting sun, then gives way to the dark in a single instant. The space around us grew bluer, and warm streetlights lit up on the boulevard.

I'll finish this beer, have a smoke, and get going, my father said. He said that he'd take the metro to Kashirskaya, then catch a cab and go out to the ring road, sleep in his truck, and load up in the morning.

I had been looking at my father, both of us seated in the middle of the bench, and failed to notice that we were now flanked by young women; two had sat down on my side and the others gathered around, so my father and I found ourselves at the center of their conversation. They were holding cans of cocktails and beer and chatting to one another as if my father and I weren't there. They laughed loudly, playfully cursing at one another. My father looked up and started eyeing them with interest.

I'd spotted them from afar; they were a group of lesbians. I could tell by the asymmetrical haircuts and the jeans worn low on the hips with wide belts. They were acting like street boys, which was also a dead giveaway—the women were mouthing off at each another, and one kept wiping her lips sharply with the sleeve of her tracksuit jacket after every sip of beer. My father watched them curiously. He didn't mind their being so rowdy right next to us, while I was irritated by the loud laughter and the entitlement with which they took up all our space. I spoke to them, saying that they'd interrupted our conversation. The women turned toward the sound of my voice and looked genuinely surprised. They apologized and said they hadn't noticed us there, then immediately moved to a neighboring bench.

My father gaped after them and with some astonishment remarked that they were a very odd group of girls, since they were acting more like guys. I told him they were lesbians. Lesbians hang out at Pushkinskaya a lot, I said. My father kept watching them, and I could see that his interest had nothing to do with anger or fear. Of course the culture he came from was homophobic, but this hatred didn't extend to gay women. My father respected and held in high esteem women who could do men's work, and those who coolly and unabashedly made use of the attributes of masculinity.

During another visit, when my friend Nastya had met us near the Domodedovskaya metro stop in her little silver Opel, he'd hopped right into the front seat, and, forgetting all else, started talking about the advantages of the model she drove, the frequency of inspections, and the cost of annual maintenance. It pleased him to talk to her about important things, things concerning the Opel. And he was flattered that a beautiful woman was chauffeuring him around Moscow in her fancy car. He relished her flirtatiousness and occasionally turned to me to ask jokingly why all my girl friends were bald. Pure coincidence, I said. Liza had always gone around with her head shaved, but Nastya had shaved hers only recently, out of some esoteric considerations.

The cut suited her. It made it easier to see her face—a vein running smoothly from her left eyebrow to her hairline, her shining gray eyes. She was gorgeous. Her vitality and fearlessness both charmed and frightened me. In spring she'd bought a turquoise retro scooter, and we liked to get loaded on vodka and drive around on it at night. In summertime she refused to wear underwear, and when the wind at high speeds blew up the broad flounces of her skirt, Nastya broke into easy, wholehearted laughter—maybe at the cool air that felt good between her legs, or at the thought that anyone who wanted to could see her vulva. Once, drunk on tequila, she tried to sleep with me, but I wasn't into the idea. I was sober, and her drunken come-on upset me. I didn't want to deal with the sad consequences of that kind of sex. Nastya rented a room between Chistye Prudy and Sukharevskaya, and I often spent the night at her place, sleeping in her bed. She had a trim, tanned body, and I liked looking at her and smelling her smell.

Before falling asleep, Nastya talked to me about her boyfriends and showed me reproductions of Renaissance paintings. She talked to me the way a young mother talks to her adult daughter. This only intensified my confusion, and something twisted inside me, strained, and gave her all the warmth I could muster. I was wholly devoted to her; she could have taken anything she wanted from me. She said that she'd dreamed that I was her daughter, and stroked the top of my head. She told me I was pretty, but I didn't believe her. I thought that she saw the entire world as beautiful because she imagined that it was. I saw the world as complicated and gray. I was afraid of the future and oppressed by the past, and because of this I was unable to feel anything in the present.

On days I didn't spend with Nastya, I lay on my bed at the dorm and stared at the ceiling. As long as my roommates were out I didn't bother turning on the light, instead watching as white daylight ran out and was replaced by an acid cobalt twilight. Since childhood I'd had a habit of looking at light. Light could not be grasped or apprehended. It was beautiful, and I didn't consider time spent watching it as wasted. I lay in my dorm room, watched the light, and felt everything inside me soften, becoming boundless and warm. Inside my belly was a pink mire that could take in everything. It consumed me, or maybe I was becoming one with it. I could sense that whatever was happening to me was what's called maturity, becoming a woman. I wanted to become a woman like Nastya, but I knew that was impossible. The thought made me feel cramped within myself. A dark evening finally arrived, and one of my roommates turned on the light without asking. She had to eat supper and read Hesiod. I was also supposed to read Hesiod. With the lights on and other people around, I couldn't become a pink mire or think of Nastya. So I turned on my laptop, went to Lib.ru, and read the *Theogony*.

My father thought of Nastya as a woman who knew how to handle a car, meaning that she was more than a woman. The group of lesbians hanging out at Pushkinskaya were women who boldly engaged in male behaviors and had sex with other women. Although they were less appealing to him than Nastya, they nevertheless commanded his interest and respect. Watching them, my father finished his now-flat beer and noted regretfully that it was hardly beer, more like sour piss. He asked if there was a curfew at my dorm, and I told him the curfew was midnight but I was going to stay at Nastya's. Hearing her name, my father perked up and insistently asked that I give her a share of the watermelons and grapes we'd bought that day. I wasn't going to argue, there were a lot of grapes, and I wasn't going to eat them all myself.

Back in the summer of 2010 we drove into Moscow. The smoke really was incredibly thick, Fyodor hadn't exaggerated. On some stretches of road there was visibility for only two meters ahead, and my father drove with his headlights on. We showered at a truck stop and changed our clothes. My father put on a light T-shirt, shorts, and plastic slides (they'd gotten filthy on the road, so he rinsed them under the faucet by the bathroom). I put on my last clean long-sleeved shirt. Over the course of a week I'd gone through all the clothes I brought with me, and now my dirty laundry sat beneath my seat in the orange bag left from the watermelon. I was too embarrassed to drive into the city in Hawaiian shorts, and they weren't fresh anyway, so I dug up my jeans and sneakers from my backpack. I had nothing else to wear on my feet. Because of a late cargo loading and poor visibility, we'd had to spend the previous night by the roadside outside the city. Too lazy to jump down from the cabin as I got ready for bed, I brushed my teeth hanging out of the window. In the process, I'd accidentally swept one of my sandals to the ground, and a dog must have run off with it, one of the dogs that lived behind a nearby stop's garbage bins. There was no one else to suspect, who else could have needed such a thing? I wandered around the garbage and the bushes by the road but failed to find the sandal. As I stalked its territory, the dog watched me nervously and quietly whined. My father thought it was hilarious that a dog had nabbed my shoe, but I was sad to lose the sandals I'd spent a long time picking out in a discount sportswear store, where I'd been very proud of finding a decent pair of shoes for two hundred and thirty rubles. For a long time after, my right sandal lay beneath the passenger seat, and whenever he drove by, my father pulled in at the stop to call and let me know he was paying a visit to my sandal thief. A few years later the dog disappeared, maybe dead of some doggy disease. Or maybe she joined a pack or moved to a more abundant dump site.

I told my father that I needed to go to the Yugo-Zapadnaya metro stop, that in the RUDN University building nearby there was an International Student Identity Card office where I could get a discounted plane ticket for my flight back. We got to the Domodedovskaya stop and went down into the metro; I kept a little insert with a map of the Moscow metro inside my passport holder. The metro car was empty. Everyone who could had left the city, and the only people going down into the metro now were workers and migrants. Looking up from the map, I saw our reflection in the window. My white shirt didn't make me look any more composed, and the long drive, the broken sleep in an awkward position, and my peculiar relationship with my father had given my face a suffering cast. My father looked sullen. His steppe-ravaged face appeared angry into the cold reflection of the window. He was staring ahead of him, lost in thought. Two drunk workers chatted cheerfully a few meters away from us, and across sat a woman wearing slides and a thick colorful dress over raspberry trousers. Next to her was a quiet little girl in a nice synthetic dress who was openly staring at me, while I looked back at her. The woman's dark eyes, fringed with thick lashes, fluttered closed. She dozed, keeping a tight grip on her daughter's shoulder. The brown metro car was cheerless. Everything in it spoke of hardship and poverty. We belonged to the class of people obliged to ride the metro and walk the city through the toxic white smog of the wildfires.

Before we'd set out, my father asked me which street the RUDN building was on, and I told him that it was on Miklukho-Maklaya Street. Ah, said my father thoughtfully, the great scientist, and he reached for the glove compartment to get his atlas of Russian roads. He paged through until he found the map of the southern part of Moscow. Murmuring to himself, he traced his finger over the page, then shut the atlas. We can walk there from the metro, he said. When we were aboveground again, my father pointed out a shopping center on the other side of the street. Let's stop by there, he said. Look, there's a bookstore, we can get a newspaper.

We walked into a Chitai-Gorod chain bookstore, and my

father started looking through the periodicals. It was the first time I'd ever seen so many books. I had come from Novosibirsk to visit my father, and in that city there was one large book-store, Kapital, but I was too shy to go in there because I wasn't sure how you were supposed to act. While I studied remotely at Novosibirsk State Tech, I was allowed to borrow books from their library, so I took advantage of that. But then I didn't show up for the first finals session and got kicked out. I downloaded pirated versions of books to my laptop; that's how I first read Eduard Limonov and Richard Bach. The literary critic Elena Makeenko also lent me books that she brought back from book fairs in Krasnoyarsk and Moscow, and it was thanks to her that I first read the cult writer Mikhail Elizarov's prose and Elena Fanailova's poetry. When I was invited to take part in poetry readings, I would wander over to the book stand at the Stray Dog bar and look at the books they were selling. I couldn't af-ford to buy any of them, but I was even more ashamed that I didn't know what to get if I could. I knew nothing about even the modest selection of books at that stand.

Why are you standing around? Pick out some books, you're the future writer, you need to have books, my father said.

I glanced around, book spines blurring before my eyes; my anxiety was making everything soft and viscous. I wasn't sure how to navigate the store, or what I was supposed to want among the multitude of choices. Variety, when you don't know what to do with it, becomes noise. My father came back over holding his newspapers.

Why are you standing there? he asked again. Go on, pick something out.

I'd always found baffling the simplicity with which he navigated spaces I perceived as alien. I turned to the register and saw that the hostility I felt was definitely not imaginary. The clerk had stood up from the chair behind her computer and was watching us attentively. She was making sure that we didn't steal. But we weren't there to steal, we just wanted to buy books and newspapers. Feeling her stare on the back of my head, I went toward a basket with a sign announcing *Sale—30% Off* and picked out two books. One was by Bernard Werber—I'd previously downloaded his dystopian sci-fi novel about ants and read it over one Sunday shift, while the café where I worked was empty, no manager and no customers. The second book was by a British Indian writer whose name I've forgotten. The book jacket said it was an autobiographical novel about an Indian woman adopted by British parents who returned to Mumbai forty years later to find her birth parents and her siblings. I brought the books quickly to the register, so the clerk wouldn't have time to suspect me of anything, and passed them to her. My father caught up with me and put his newspapers on top of my stack. He stood next to me, unaware of the clerk's judgmental gaze, and dug unhurriedly through his pockets for coins, so she wouldn't need to make change. He had come to the bookstore to buy a few books and papers, and that's exactly what he was doing. We took the brand-name bag the clerk offered and put the books and newspapers inside. I used that bag for a long time after—it was solidly made and well suited to storing my toothpaste, toothbrush, and razor.

When we left the shopping center, my father lit a cigarette, looking around. I was trying not to smoke in Moscow; the smog made my head spin, and my throat was constantly going dry. We're going there, my father said, pointing in the direction we were supposed to take. He threw his butt into a trash can, and we walked that way. He steered me across avenues, through court-yards, and down streets, but we weren't walking at random—he'd memorized the map. Having looked at it carefully in the morning, he kept it in his mind, the way the little blue navigator arrow crawls across a screen. We passed tightly shut windows and empty sidewalk cafés. At one particular café, my father no-ticed the chalkboard on the grass. He read the chalked word aloud—Mo-ji-to—and turned to me. What's that? he asked.

I said it was a cold cocktail made with soda water, mint, and ice. That's an ad for a nonalcoholic one, but usually it's made with rum.

Interesting, my father said. After we get the tickets, let's have one of those mojitos.

A few blocks from RUDN we came across another café mak-ing mojitos and decided to try that one. My father liked that the café had a patio where we could sit in the shade and smoke; that's what he said.

I said that the smoke everywhere was drowning out the light, and if there's no light, there's no shade either. My father raised his head to look at the sky. It was gray, and in the center a flat white saucer barely shone.

Yes, he confirmed, look at that, can't even see the sun.

On the way back from RUDN we went into the café he'd pointed out, and a young server in a starched white shirt and brown apron came out to the patio to meet us. The sight of us stunned her, but she greeted us, reluctantly, anyway. I asked for a menu and an ashtray; my father immediately lit a cigarette. I opened the heavy menu in its faux-leather binder and found a list of summer drinks. The server was standing by the bar, keeping an eye on us. I waved her over and asked for two nonalcoholic mojitos. She disappeared, and my father asked me to pass him one of the newspapers from the bag. A quarter of an hour passed. On the patio across from us sat a sterile young man in spotless white sneakers and a tightly knotted tie, starting intently at his little MacBook. On his table stood a plate holding an unfinished club sandwich and a large teapot. I'd worked in a café for two years by then, so I knew that it took no longer than three minutes to make a mojito. The server likely hadn't put in our order and was just waiting for us to go away. I didn't want to relay my suspicions to my father, because I didn't want him to know what was happening. I got up, found the server, and reminded her about our drinks. I'm not sure why, but I wanted to protect him from the ire and mistrust she clearly felt for us. Maybe I felt responsible—I was now the one showing him the world I knew, after all. I was the one who could say what went into a mojito. He knew the world of roadside cafés, where it didn't matter who you were or what you looked like; those places fed everyone who could pay. The injustice here was that we were perfectly capable of paying for our drinks, but we were not believed, and were despised.

I returned quickly to our table. The ashtray was already overflowing with my father's cigarette butts, while he himself was calmly reading an article about the fires and smog blanketing Moscow. Three minutes later the server came out to the patio; she was carrying two tall glasses of ice and mint on a tray, each glass with two straws. Along with the drinks she'd brought our check, placing it demonstratively on the table. She didn't leave after putting the glasses down, either, but stood there waiting for us to pay. I understood this right away and asked my father to get his wallet. One mojito cost two hundred and fifty rubles, and my father took out a five-hundred-ruble bill and put it in the cardboard check holder. I asked the server to bring us a new ashtray, and she, satisfied, brought us two. I explained to my father that a mojito comes with two straws, a wide one and a narrow one. The main straw is the narrow one, while the wide straw is there in case the narrow straw gets blocked by mint leaves and ice. My father put aside his newspaper and took a sip. Sweet, he said, and immediately drained all the liquid in his glass. He looked at my glass and asked what we were supposed to do with the ice and whether it was honest to make drinks that were almost entirely ice, anyway.

I said it was a reasonable question, but a mojito was supposed to be drunk slowly, so that the ice melted gradually as you drank. It's a refreshing cocktail for the beach, I said.

Whatever you say, my father said. It's definitely not worth two fifty.

Like a lot of other things, I said.

That's all of fucking Moscow for you, my father said thoughtfully. Let's have one more smoke and get going to the stop. Tomorrow night I have to be in Tambov.

17

After his funeral I went to Crimea to see my mother. Late September was stormy, and the peninsula had lost its color. Summer had singed the green from the grass, and in the cold wind the water had a leaden hue. Everything was gray or beige, like a homely day of mourning. My great-aunt Masha, Minnegel-apa, sat in her armchair monitoring the evening news. She was particularly concerned with the forecast, because the last storm had killed several people—a great wave had swept them from the pier and pulled them into the open sea. My great-aunt mourned for them; she pitied the people who'd died such a pointless death. All they'd wanted was to take a picture of the sea, and it had devoured them. With her glasses on, listening to the local news channel, Aunt Masha kept repeating one thing—their deaths had been so unfair. And then, remembering the reason we were gathered in her house, she would turn and look for a long time at my face. Noticing, I responded to her gaze with a questioning gesture. And Masha, grumbling something to herself, would say to me that I had to take care of my father's posthumous business and then, when the time came, return to Astrakhan to find out why he'd died so young. I nodded obediently. I already knew why he had died, but I couldn't bring myself to tell her that.

My mother sat in another armchair, also watching television. Seated next to each other, the two of them looked like Tatar nesting dolls, both with matte brown eyes like wet chestnuts, upturned pointed noses, sizable square jaws. They sat beneath a portrait gallery of Minnegel-apa's siblings. The photographs on the right were of dark-eyed, red-haired men and women; to the left hung the gray-eyed blonds. After the birth of Grandpa Rafik and the death of Minnegel and Rafik's mother, their father, Mirdjan, had married a Russian woman. Minnegel kept her eyes on the screen, running her sturdy dark fingers through the fringe of the armchair cover. She never talked about her faith, though she often said that Mirdjan had been a well-respected man in Chistopol; he knew the Quran by heart and recited beautifully. The kids were forbidden to stay in the house when neighbors came to see him, asking him to slaughter a lamb or circumcise a boy, but as a child Minnegel would hide beneath the window and listen to her father's voice. Now she sat there in a turban fashioned out of white cotton fabric, which is what she always wore at home. She never showed her hair, and I had seen it down only once, by accident, one night when she walked into the room where I was sleeping to shut the windows thrown open by a gust of wind. Dyed light brown, her hair reached down to her heels. During the day she plaited it into a few thin braids, relying on bobby pins and clips to twist the braids into a voluminous nest.

Minnegel had never had children. Soviet oncologists had removed her ovaries and her uterus, and Minnegel—the oldest daughter, who'd grown up raising her younger brother, my grandfather Rafik—spent the rest of her life caring for Rafik as though he were a chronically ill child. And he was that, a sick child: he had been an alcoholic since his youth and suffered from bouts of groundless rage. He beat his first wife, my grandmother Valentina, nearly to death, and later also beat his second wife, another Valentina. Whenever the women pulled themselves together and threw him out of the house, he went back to his sister. She took him in as an orphan. Their mother had died of pneumonia during the war, before Rafik was one, so nine-year-old Minnegel had become his mother. It was a close, stifling relationship, in which she went along with his every whim and at the same time judged him harshly for it. Her love for him was born of pity, and he remained a silly little boy far into his old age. But he really was a mean man. I met Rafik for the first time a few years before my father's death: his alcohol-ravaged face still held the traces of handsome, masculine Tatar features. He lived in a banya across the road from Minnegel's house, and when he was sober he fed the hens and chopped wood. Drunk, he would vomit into a basin that stood by his *tapchan*; his ulcers, and later his stomach cancer, made untroubled drinking impossible, but he still got drunk every chance he could.

When I sat down next to my mother and Minnegel-apa, it was easy to see the Tatar blood washing out of us, generation after generation. Although it retains some Tatar features, my face looks entirely Russified. On my mother's birth certificate, Rafik Mirdjanovich Muzafarov is registered as Tatar, while my grandmother Valentina Ivanovna Zobnina appears as Russian, and my grandfather registered their daughter, Angella Rafikovna Muzafarova, as Russian, too. So we were Russian, and it was easier for everyone to call Rafik Roman, while Minnegel became Masha. It was Rafik who'd decided to name my mother Angella, after the Black lesbian feminist activist Angela Davis. My father had been named Yuriy after Yuriy Gagarin. My father used to make fun of my mother, jokingly calling her *tatarva*, Tatar trash. He understood her Tatar heritage as a kind of congenital flaw, an accident of fate. My mother disliked her Tatar features, but with the years her face became sharper and flattened out broad and square, like Minnegel's.

My mother first visited Minnegel twenty years after Grandfather Rafik came to Crimea. In 1989, Grandma Valentina finally plucked up the courage to declare that my mother had to choose which of her parents she wanted at her wedding. My mother asked my grandfather Rafik not to come. He bought tickets and went to his sister's. Rafik was emotionally unreachable and almost always drunk. On her first Crimean visit, my mother brought him a gift: a short-sleeved shirt and some thermal underwear. He wore these until he died—not out of sentimentality, I thought, but just out of regular male pragmatism: the shirt and thermals were there to be worn, not much else to it. My mother and grandfather didn't know how to talk to each other; my mother kept cracking little jokes at his expense, while he grew helplessly, childishly furious at her insolence. I didn't have much to say to my grandfather, either: when he saw me for the first time, he seized me tightly with bony fingers and started making odd complaints about my height, saying I was somehow a little too healthy. I wasn't even particularly large; he was just a short, sinewy old man, surprised and bothered by my youth and strength. Letting go of me, he sat down on the sofa, and I sat next to him. Grandfather Rafik turned his expressionless face to me for a moment, but almost immediately looked away again and stared at the television. We sat there for five minutes or so, until he got up anxiously, telling me to straighten the sofa cover, took a plate of freshly baked *piroshki* from the kitchen, and left the house.

I remained a bit afraid of him and preferred talking to Minnegel's husband, my great-uncle Vitya, a kindly agronomist who until the final days of the Soviet Union had managed grape and tobacco farms in the Crimean south. When Uncle Vitya learned that I was studying at the Gorky Literary Institute, he developed a great deal of respect for me. For him, someone who wrote could only be an "honest correspondent." He proudly told me the story of a young journalist who had come to one of his farms to interview him, proceeded to get drunk on the local Kagor wine, and accidentally went to Sevastopol instead of Simferopol, then published his piece in a Moscow newspaper and sent Uncle Vitya a clipping of it by mail. I tried to explain that I wasn't studying journalism, but Uncle Vitya couldn't hear me, because he was practically deaf. He spent his days seated on a stool, holding the sides of a large television topped with a snow-white doily, and watching soccer matches and the news, with one ear held against the speaker. At dinner he'd raise his glass of fruit liqueur, turn to me, and say: what do you say, correspondent, shall we?

When Vitya and Minnegel were assigned to work in Crimea in the seventies, the administration of Yalta gave them a small apartment in the mountains, with a plot of rocky mountain soil for a garden. Minnegel used it to grow sweet green figs and strawberries. Once, when I was visiting, she handed me a plastic bucket and told me to bring it to Uncle Vitya in the orchard.

He'd gone to pick berries and forgot to bring the bucket along. I went down a steep staircase carved into the rock and squeezed through a gap in the hedge. Uncle Vitya was sitting on the slope in his ancient, faded white Panama bucket hat, and looking out over the tree line in the direction where, beyond the hills, the sea began. There was no way for him to hear me. He sat in the deep silence of his deafness, thinking something to himself. The scene made me sad—I couldn't imagine what might occupy the mind of this quiet, jovial old man. I could hear the chirring of crickets as the waves of their songs rose above the tangled grass, one after another. The sky was a piercing blue. The fierce southern light dazzled my eyes. I came closer to Uncle Vitya and heard that he was singing quietly—a feeble, sad little tune. He was sunk in melancholy, looking out over the trees.

I didn't know what I was supposed to do: I couldn't leave the bucket and go back to the house, because then he'd know that I had been watching him; interrupting his singing, on the other hand, would be a rude intrusion on my part. I sat down some distance away from him to wait for the end of his solitary meditation. Sitting there, I thought that all of old age must be like this lonely gaze into the distance, a gaze toward something unreachable. A solitary disappointment and an internal audit, and a kind of nostalgia for the world you'll soon be obliged to leave. An unbearable longing for the future and an impotent rage at a world that will remain the same even without you in it. We sat on the stony slope, and I watched as he swayed his head and ran his right hand over the dry grass by his hip. He was alone here, and the wild, restless world capered around him. Uncle Vitya fascinated me, and I began to feel that I wasn't watching him from a short distance away but in some other context, like, maybe, in a movie. Then I wasn't thinking about him at all but looking over the treetops myself, imagining the world as a vast place filled with life, when he abruptly turned around. I started in surprise and managed an embarrassed smile; remembering his poor eyesight, I raised my arm in a friendly wave. Uncle Vitya was looking at me with anger. I motioned toward the bucket, and he gave a restrained nod. I stood, pointing toward the bucket once more, and backed up toward the hedge. He nodded in acknowledgment and turned away. Climbing hurriedly through a gap in the growth, I scraped my legs, and the thin pink scratches began immediately to burn. I was unsettled by the dark look he had given me. Did he know that I'd intruded on his solitude, ruined his moment of sublime sorrow? Or had he been thinking about something he truly hated? The old sorcerer on the mountainside frightened me, and at supper that evening I tried not to look in his direction.

On my final visit I was just passing through, spending only a few days at their house. They were all still alive then. Preparing to depart, I sat down on the warm wooden porch to lace up my sneakers and heard Uncle Vitya moving slowly, leaning on his cane, as he left the house. He wasn't going out to the orchard anymore by then; his legs were getting weaker. He only came into the yard to wipe down his yellow Zaporozhets and rest for a while on the bench beneath the old chestnut tree. It was difficult for Uncle Vitya to walk, and out of respect for his effort, I stopped rushing. He came out and settled on the bench next to me with a loud groan. I shifted to give him more space and turned to face him, smiling. He was staring at me very closely, though his gaze seemed to be directed at something far away.

He looked at me with his ancient eyes, blinking slowly. Uncle Vitya reminded me of a giant koala. I wasn't going to hurry him along, but I also wasn't sure why he had come out to sit with me. Five minutes earlier, I'd gone into his bedroom and stood in a spot where he could see me, pointing at my backpack. He took one look and turned away, waving me off. Now he'd caught up with me and sat breathing loudly, so I couldn't bring myself to get up—I felt that he'd come out to see me for some particular reason, that there was something he wanted to say to me. We both sat looking ahead, and after some time had gone by he began to speak, but his voice lacked the merriment with which he'd toasted his honest correspondent; neither did it have the intensity of his laments about the wasted tobacco fields. All the surface layers of his intonation were gone, and I was listening to a calm, measured old man. He told me that I was a rare type of woman. I haven't seen many others like you, he said. You're a wandering woman, there's no peace anywhere for a woman like you. You always have to be going somewhere, running from something. All most women want is to make a home, but you need something else, you're homeless and you see this homelessness not as a lack but as the only way to live. You're not interested in men, and you don't need them, either. It's going to be hard going for you, he concluded.

I had been listening to him with my entire body, and when he finished I tried to smile again, but all I could do was give an awkward, lopsided shrug. In any case, he wasn't looking at me any longer—leaning on his walking stick, he heaved himself up noisily, clapped me on the back with his broad dry palm, and walked away. His words had left me with a bitter feeling. The bitterness spread along my arms and legs, throughout my chest. What he said had exposed me—and, at the same time, it had brought me a terrible joy.

Now I was in Crimea to see my mother. She hadn't come to my father's funeral. When I asked her why, she said with distaste that she didn't want to see his mother, her ex-mother-in-law, and I didn't bring it up again after that. At night we lay in a little bedroom, side by side on a bed made up with a feather quilt, and talked quietly about the day. Then she'd fall asleep while I went on lying there in the dark, looking at the cold glow of the whitewashed ceiling and the thin tapestry depicting two proud deer, which wavered slightly in the currents of air. On the day I arrived, Minnegel-apa had opened a few bottles of wine and made kasha and mayonnaise salad; drunk and sated, everyone had wandered back to their rooms, and only my mother and I could not fall asleep. We sat savoring our cigarettes and talking in the dark shadow of the old chestnut tree. The air smelled of cooling leaves. A single cigarette wasn't enough, and each of us lit another. The orange ember of my mother's slim cigarette flickered and flared. We threw the stubs into a jar of water that Minnegel-apa had given my mother. She didn't like for women to smoke, but my mother had whiningly reminded her that she was forty-four years old. I'd been waiting for this moment all day, and now I finally said to my mother that my father's meningitis was a consequence of AIDS. I told her I was worried about her HIV status; I asked if she and my father had used protection when they lived together. My mother exhaled noisily—she was smoking a sweetish Glamour—and replied that my father had insisted on condoms himself. Even before he died, she said, I went to the doctor with a yeast infection and they ran all the tests, my HIV test was negative. My mother seemed unmoved, and I was shocked by the cold superiority with which she talked about my father. She couldn't share in my anxiety, my disorientation. At the time I thought of her indifference as betrayal.

$$-\ 18\ -$$

[The] consequence is abandonment.

—SUSAN SONTAG

When your father dies of AIDS, it's not like he's died of heart failure or a stroke. The word *AIDS* alone brings on a vague sense of shame. I saw my father a year before he died: his face was partly paralyzed, and he dragged one leg behind him when he walked. In the picture on his renewed commercial driver's license, he looked like a withered old man: his yellowish eyes, the color of river silt, were dull, or maybe they reflected the flash of the camera. To conceal his cause of death, Ilona put aside all his cheating and took charge of his documents and the funeral. She hid all documentation of his HIV status. I arrived in Astrakhan in a state of confusion—my father had called me from the hospital three days before his death and bragged that he'd trained the nurses to wipe down the windowsills thrice a day. He thought they were lazy, and in his own words claimed to have *run them through the drills*.

Two weeks before he died, he'd been hospitalized with a severe headache. He was driving empty from Astrakhan to Volgograd, and one morning he felt that something was not right with his head and took some paracetamol. But halfway through the drive the pain became so intense that he barely made it to the nearest motel, from which he called Fyodor. Luckily, Fyodor was in Astrakhan then; he called in some other guys, and they came to get my father in someone's car. They put him in the back seat and drove him back to Astrakhan. They came back for his truck the following day. In the hospital, pumped full of painkillers, my father quickly felt like himself again and couldn't understand why they wouldn't let him go home. But he was most outraged by the state of the room he'd been put in; he was in the most neglected wing of the infectious disease ward, with other HIV-positive men, and every day he saw these men, one by one, taken out in black body bags.

The first intensification of his illness had come a year before he died, but, naturally, he paid it no attention. Knowing my father, I can say with certainty that he wasn't registered anywhere, certainly not with the regional AIDS center. He was aware of his status and thought of it as something fatal. HIV seemed to my father to be a common illness that was somehow supposed to kill him. But he didn't know when this would happen, and so all his days became a cycle of recurring deathbed moments. At some point the cycle would end, and he accepted this fact with resentment and sorrow.

I discovered by accident that he had died of AIDS. Talking to Ilona, I implied that I was determined to find out what had killed him. Meningitis, I knew, was treatable. It was very strange for a grown man to have died of that. Ilona went pale, and, taking me by the sleeve, pulled me into their bedroom, where in a rapid-fire whisper she told me what had happened. She looked directly at me and barely blinked. The light in the room was dark blue, like night is in the steppe. Ilona's eyes seemed iridescent in that light. She was afraid. She was afraid of ignorant gossip, afraid that she would die. And she was unbearably ashamed. The vulnerability I became privy to that night was that of a woman who had done nothing wrong, but didn't realize it. I listened to her without interrupting, but it was difficult to be with her. From hysterical whispering she switched to obsequious babbling. Begging for forgiveness, she told me that she'd fed my father well and given him his vitamins. Remember, she said to me, I was always telling him to take his vitamins. I do remember that, I said, hoping to calm her; I didn't want to feel that she was somehow guilty. Because she wasn't guilty of anything. She'd given my father vitamins, but vitamins weren't going to help. My father led a destructive way of life: he was always on the road, hardly slept, smoked two packs a day, and once every two weeks drank himself unconscious. A few times I'd seen him smoking weed in the breaks between routes, or during a long session of loading cargo.

I asked Ilona to leave and remained alone in the blue room, not turning on the light. Sitting down on the side of the large bed bought at some point in the past by my father, I remembered how during a two-week break between routes, some truckers had brought him home. He hadn't passed out, but he wasn't conscious, either; he was in a state Ilona called *the mumbles*. Four men carried him up the stairs to the sixth floor, and behind his body trailed a dotted line of thick droplets of blood. According to the guys, he had stood up to go to his truck and immediately fell facedown onto a concrete curb. Inside the apartment they put him on the sofa. His face and clothes were drenched in blood. The smell of alcohol filled the room: Ilona rushed over with a half-liter bottle of disinfectant, spreading her arms and scowling, and ordered everyone to get away from him. All four men backed up and left the apartment without saying goodbye. We were on our own, and I wanted to help Ilona, but she waved me away sharply and ordered me not to touch my father. Back then I had taken her behavior for a show of care, but now I understood that she was afraid the blood from his open wound would get on me and the men. She soaked a piece of gauze in disinfectant and put it to my father's mangled nose. He howled with pain, like a wild animal caught in a snare. He writhed on the sofa, while Ilona, grasping his shoulders, pressed him into the pillow and refused to let him rise. When he passed out, she soaked more gauze in alcohol, wiped the blood from the floor, blotted the stains on the rug. Having finished, she sighed with relief and tossed the gauze into the trash. All this time I'd been sitting on the step that divided the balcony from the room and watching my roaring drunk father thrash on the colorful fringed bedspread. The room had become narrow and close with the smells of alcohol and fresh blood and the cloudy aroma of mallow flowers mixed with the smells of fuel oil and male sweat. The lamp's warm light fell on Ilona's brown skin. I felt shame and unbearable pity for all of us, that we had wound up here. There was no power that could reverse what was happening. There was no instrument to slice away a section of time and space and, wrapping them in a piece of paper, toss them out, the farther the better, someplace over the fence.

Watching my father, I thought I understood him. I could feel that inside me there was something that could not be fed to satisfaction; it was like a darkness that begged only to be destroyed. Where was the border between this darkness and my self? I couldn't say. I knew the feeling that drove my father—he was moved by the desire to leave himself behind. After a hard seventeen-hour shift at the café where I worked, I would come home, pull my pants down to my ankles, and sit like that for a long time, feeling some slight relief. The denim was heavy and permeated with the odors of coffee oils and the kitchen, my crotch and my sweat; on the inside of the pant legs I could see bits of dry skin. I stared at my jeans, and I smelled them. I often wanted to step out of myself the way I stepped out of my work pants. I wanted to take off all of me. The same thing went on with my father—being alone with himself or not being on the road was unendurable for him. There was a darkness in him, but this darkness didn't make him a romantic hero or someone to be pitied and saved. The darkness deformed him and turned the world around us—me, him, Ilona—into a cramped space where all of us suffered.

I found out about his death early in the morning.

Two weeks before, I'd made a fake dorm pass for my lover

Veronika. Just before the doors closed for the night she'd show it to the guard and go up to see me on the fourth floor. We slept on my narrow bed, without pillows, beneath a thin sheet. I believed then that living ascetically could help me understand the way the world worked and help with my anxiety attacks. But nothing happened the way I intended. At night, after a day of strict fasting, I would binge eat and get drunk on cheap champagne and beer, then find myself unable to sleep because I was so uncomfortable and cold. Veronika slept at the edge of the bed, rolling up her jacket beneath her cheek. When she was asleep I looked at her head, which she, too, shaved bald. I liked her eyes and her thick eyelids, fringed with dark lashes. Her lips folded into a pouty cupid's bow. In the September morning light everything looked large, clearly contoured, bright. Even the hideousness of my dorm room, with its standard-issue vinyl wallpaper and brown linoleum, looked purposeful. I didn't want to get up. As always, I had slept through the lectures on economics and the theory of literary criticism, but I could still make it to art history, which I tried never to miss. I climbed over sleeping Veronika, who smelled like a light hangover and earthy sweat, and went to the fridge, on top of which lay my white Nokia. I saw seven missed calls from Ilona and three from my mother. The calls began at 5:30 a.m., which meant they'd been trying to reach me for five hours. In the Incoming Calls list I selected my mother and pressed Dial. She picked up right away, and with some difficulty, as though she were speaking to me from the bottom of a deep well, said that last night my father had died. I was silent; she asked me what I was going to do. I would get on the train today and go to the funeral. I asked her whether she would go, and she remained silent for a moment, then said she hadn't made up her mind.

I bought a ticket for the evening train. Veronika came to see me off, but she didn't know what she was supposed to do in this situation and kept smiling awkwardly. I didn't know how I was supposed to behave, either. My father had died young, he was only forty-seven. Three days earlier, he'd been shouting at me on the phone that he'd really give the staff at that ward something to remember him by. Now he was in a black bag in a section of the hospital refrigerator. When he was moved from intensive care to the infectious disease ward, he was appalled by its shabbiness and the disregard for the people there: yellowed plaster hung down from the ceiling in wide strips, and mattresses lay moldering in their frames, the stuffing in them clumped. He took a short video on his Samsung of the conditions in which sick people were kept. For the entire thirty seconds of the video, shot with a shaky hand, of the yellow ward with its rotting walls and exposed beams, you can hear his furious cursing. He called Ilona and demanded that she post the video online so that everyone could see how patients at the city hospital were being treated. I found his insistence touching; it was predicated on an understanding of the internet as one large, Soviet-era community bulletin board.

He didn't understand that his video, like many others that wind up online, would sink to the bottom of the internet, where no one would see it. He spoke scathingly of the on-duty nurses. He understood that the misery he had encountered was systemic in nature, but he couldn't help taking out his rage on the junior medical staff. I tried to stick up for the nurses, but this made him even angrier, and he started blaming everything on me. I listened wordlessly as he cursed, and when he was finished, I quietly pronounced: *Go fuck yourself then.*

Now nothing could bother him or make him indignant. He lay in darkness, his skull had been sawed open from ear to ear. I paid the conductor for a set of sheets and took them out of the bag, making up the lumpy mattress, then hopping up into the top bunk. It was a beautiful day, and I was seeing it through a clear soundproof wall. The snow-white sheets of the woman with whom I shared the compartment billowed like an iceberg; she sat on her blanket, slowly drinking tea from a glass and crying. When she put the tea glass holder down on the table, it began jangling quietly. Noticing, she moved it to her knees. She kept getting calls and delivered brief updates quietly into the phone: her mother had died, she was going to bury her. We were the train's mourning car.

Tired of watching this woman, I lay down on my back and started crying, too. I was crying out of utter bewilderment and fear. I was afraid to see my father dead. I had a fear of funerals and of corpses. When I was in high school, several of my friends had died. These were sudden, inexplicable deaths: a suicide, acute leukemia, one guy who got caught on a piece of driftwood while swimming and drowned. I went to their funerals but tried to avoid looking inside the caskets. I could smell the oppressive aroma of the flowers, the damp dead body, the ceremonial *kutia*. I felt repulsed by everything that had to do with the funeral ceremony. At the wakes, I tried not to touch the food. I imagined that everything on the table was part of the corpse, steeped in the juices of the dead. To be polite, I wet my lips with *kissel* and tried to ignore the chicken gone cold on my plate. Now I had to attend my father's funeral, where I would need to kiss him, because I was his daughter.

My father's death, like the deaths of my friends, was strange and incomprehensible. I felt sorry for him and bitter that he had died suddenly. At the same time, I felt a wicked sense of relief. I had experienced my father as a burden. I tried to keep our phone calls as infrequent as possible, and though out of boredom he'd call me when his cargo was being unloaded, our conversations were empty and tedious. Sometimes he called drunk and bellowed into the phone that he loved me. Thoughts of my father made me want to disappear.

I had seen how quickly he was aging, and I knew that soon he'd have to stop working as a long-haul trucker. He'd already tried driving a grocery truck within city limits. He explained this life change by saying that the long-distance routes had tired him out, he could barely move one of his arms, and one of his legs also. Driving a truck in that kind of shape was dangerous, he understood that. After a month of hauling vegetables he called Raisa again and said he could take on intercity cargo. In the city, surrounded by scampering, pesky little sedans or stuck in traffic jams, he felt stifled. He was surrounded by buildings, the steppe hidden from sight. By his second week driving in the city he began to miss all that space, and then he quit.

I dreaded the day when he would have to stop driving. That meant Ilona, or my mother, would no longer have any use for him. And since a quarter of his salary went to support his own elderly mother, it would mean that my father and my grandmother, both of them disabled, would live in poverty. The little money that made its way to me, a few thousand from every route, I spent on books and clothes, and although the help was a not insignificant addition to my student stipend and occasional paid gigs, it didn't bother me that he wouldn't be able to send me money. I could always work for it. I was afraid that no longer working as a long-distance trucker would have an effect on his entire being—his life could easily become one endless bender. And what if his arms and legs totally gave out? He wouldn't be able to move, would lie there motionless until he died. I scared myself, thinking this way. I had already started imagining that if something were to happen to him, I would have to drop out of the institute and find a full-time job so I could feed my father and care for him. I always assumed the worst, anticipated terrible consequences, because I knew that it was rare for good things to happen, and when they did, they were immediately lost to worry and routine. I thought of my paralyzed father lying in front of the TV with a face like an evil idol. Lying there with dark thoughts drifting through his mind.

And now this uncertain future had turned to nothing. It was gone. I felt relieved, and ashamed of my relief. I cried, staring at the baggage rack hanging above me, thinking that my mother, though she'd promised to consider it, would not come to the funeral. She could be in Astrakhan in five hours if she took the train, but it was obvious that she wasn't planning on going anywhere. I lay surrounded by absolute silence. News of my father's death had deafened me.

My grandmother knew what had killed my father. He'd told her about his diagnosis when she came to visit him. They sat down near the hospital entrance—he couldn't make it any farther, he didn't have the strength. A doctor had told him that this might be his last conversation with his mother. And so it was. But my grandmother refused to believe that my father could have gotten HIV himself or transmitted it to Ilona. She'd always defended him—even at school, when he beat up a classmate, she wouldn't believe the principal, accusing him of slander. She was, in every way, the mother of *blatnoy* song, and she blamed everything on Ilona. She knew all the details of Ilona's private life before she met my father. Ilona may have told her herself: two of her previous partners had died, one after the other. My grandmother saw Ilona's self-interest and deciphered it as feminine greed.

On the seventh day after my father's death I was washing the floors of her apartment for the third time at her request. The evening news shrieked from the TV. I was frustrated with her, because I'd never liked doing chores and now I was having to run around with a washrag several times a day. But along with my frustration I felt an urge to please her; after all, she'd lost her beloved son. I barely knew the woman—when I was five I'd been brought to Astrakhan for the entire summer, but according to her stories, all I did was cry because I missed my mother. She said that I'd sat on the steps of my great-grandfather's house, tearfully petting the old outdoor cat who wasn't allowed past the threshold, saying that Vaska the cat was the only one who understood me. Vaska had no mother or father, he was on his own, and I was on my own, too, without my mother. She and my great-grandfather, her father, had tried to soothe my childhood melancholy, but there was nothing they could do to help. And I don't remember that pain at all. I just remember Granddad's sheds and the summer kitchen, where while playing "bear family" I washed my grandmother's white dress in a tub of sand, water, and chicken droppings. I was having fun, holding the dress up above the tub of my mess and singing a song about me, a lady bear, washing my little daughter bear's dress. The dress would be clean as river sand, and my daughter beautiful as a queen. When I was a child I thought that anything involving water couldn't be dirty, and was always baffled by my mother's vigorous cleaning of the bathroom floor, and by the fact that my grandmother's dress was ruined after this.

It was my grandmother who insisted I be baptized, and when my father came to pick me up, we were baptized together on the same day. Then my father came down with tonsillitis, and we went to the hospital every day to visit him. There was no money for the bus, so we woke up early and walked through the old Astrakhan cemetery. Every morning we chose a new route in order to look at the elaborate monuments, the alabaster angels and grieving women. We explored the cemetery like a large outdoor museum, and I felt no fear of death; the cemetery seemed to have no connection to it. My grandmother had told me that after my baptism I would be saved.

After my parents' divorce she stopped calling, and I no longer knew anything about her life. I also had no idea how to relate to the elderly. Valentina, my grandmother on my mother's side, didn't like me, so I practically never saw her, and there weren't any other older people in my life. In the immediate aftermath of my father's death, I found myself forced to share an apartment with a virtual stranger. I listened to her patiently, forcing myself to nod and smile when I had nothing to say. All I really wanted was to be alone. I managed a few times to get out for a walk around an amusement park near the house. I paced the paved paths, my whole body tingling with anxiety because I'd left my grandmother alone. After making a few loops, seeing and hearing absolutely nothing, I returned to her apartment feeling bitterly guilty for abandoning her for thirty minutes. I berated myself for promising to stay until the ninth day after my father's death. My grandmother, meanwhile, alternated between moaning and calling for my father and sweetly asking me to wash the floors.

At night she hardly slept, nodding off for half an hour before waking up again and wandering through the apartment, whining something piteously to herself. If she couldn't sleep, I couldn't sleep, either. Dawn came early, and I got up to watch her shows with her and discuss the recommendations of the host, Dr. Yelena Malysheva, whom my grandmother trusted unconditionally. One day on the way to the cemetery, worn out by heat and lack of sleep, I responded sharply to some nonsense of hers, and she threw a fit; pretending to lose her way, she wandered into a four-lane road full of passing cars. I caught up with her, grabbing her scrawny shoulder and dragging her back to the pedestrian crossing. Back home, she pretended that she was suddenly losing her sight and went through the room wearing only her underwear, leaning on the walls for support. All of it—her feeble gait, thin, faded skin, the cotton underwear bunching on her old bottom—was supposed to make me feel intensely guilty. And I did feel guilty about upsetting my grandmother. I didn't really know her, so when I addressed her I used the formal *you*. My father had been bound to her, entirely subject to her will, but his devotion had a simple basis—it stemmed from a son's love for his mother. It was harder for her to deal with me, because I didn't like her, and after that first fit, I also stopped trusting her. And I resented that she hadn't bothered to ask how I felt about my father's passing. All the time I spent with her was devoted to her loss, leaving no room for my grief, rendering me a reflective surface for her emotions. I pitied, loathed, feared her. And repressing all of that, I began each day by dusting and changing the newspapers that covered every surface in her home—the dining table, the stand in the hall, the console beneath the television. The chairs also had to be lined with fresh papers. After dusting and changing the papers, I'd fill a bucket with water and washing liquid and get to mopping the floors, then wiping them dry with a clean rag. While I worked, she sat on her bed, and one morning when I was making my way toward her to mop by her feet, she lifted her soles and spoke in a quiet, clear voice, looking at the wall: *I know why Yura died.*

She'd weighed the facts alongside her maternal intuition and was now able to conclude that Ilona had wanted my father dead and had finally pulled it off. And I, bewildered by his death and my exhausting existence with this manipulative old woman, gave in to her. She succeeded in dragging me into her schemes. My grandmother had become convinced that Ilona profited off my father's funeral. She asked me to call the funeral home to clarify exactly how much the grave at Trusovskoye Cemetery had cost, and then to call Ilona and discreetly find out the same thing. According to my grandmother's calculations, Ilona had been able to skim twenty thousand rubles of the funeral money and split her take with the funeral agent. You know, I find it disturbing now that I allowed myself to believe her. It's true that Ilona was a complicated woman, but even if she had taken those twenty thousand, I think it would have been a kind of moral compensation. Yet, at the time, the fact of my father's death required that I find someone to blame. I hated Ilona, because my father, like any dead person, was irreproachable. It was my responsibility to defend him, because he could no longer defend himself. There was no longer anything he could do.

The morning after my conversation with Ilona in the blue room was the funeral. There was a lot to get done—pick up the wreaths, take some certificates from one place and bring them to another, escort my grandmother to the bank. Ilona said that she'd wake me at six to accompany her and my grandmother on their errands. There was no point in having me there, but I assumed that my grandmother was micromanaging Ilona and I was supposed to distract her. For a long time I was unable to fall asleep, my grandmother's loud moaning audible in the next room. In the steppe, the wind had picked up, and now it came into the city; the trees beyond my windows rustled, and the house shook. I dropped off briefly and had a dream: with his head thrown back slightly and his legs bent, my father lay on the steppe sand. He wasn't asleep, he was dead. He wore, as always, cotton slacks and a light, neatly ironed sand-colored shirt with short sleeves and a pocket. The wind raged and ruffled the grasses, but my father's body seemed untouchable. There was a clamor, the noise of the wind blending with the shouts of a marketplace. I listened intently to the voices carried on the wind; they were shouting my father's name. They were the voices of women and children, and they were calling: *Yura, Yura, Yura.* I looked closely and saw that his breast pocket and the pockets of his pants were filled to bursting with money. The din of voices was growing closer, louder, intolerable, the steppe was roiling its sands and fitfully rustling the beige grass. My father's body, previously far from the cries and the wind, was suddenly within their reach, and I saw dozens of trembling, grasping arms reaching toward him. They grabbed at his shirt, pulled him in different directions, the longest had aimed for his pockets and were scooping out handfuls of crumpled bills. They wanted to tear my father apart. I tried to stop them; I felt sorry for his body, they were going to desecrate it, and there was nothing he could do to resist. Struggling, I tried to close the gap between us, to fight off these grasping hands and arms, but I didn't have the strength, and that's when I began to scream—quietly at first, as though into a pillow, but then my voice broke through the depths of sleep and rang out in the blue room. I opened my eyes, the screams from my dream echoing in my ears. Ilona came in to ask what had happened, and I told her I'd had a nightmare. She brought me a glass of water and along the way hung my black linen dress, ironed the night before, on the wardrobe. She said that my grandmother had asked her to remove it from the hallway: she couldn't stand the sight of my mourning clothes.

At the cemetery, near the coffin, I stood watching other people approach my father's body to say goodbye. Funeral decorum says otherwise. Immediate family members are supposed to say their farewells first, and after them, everyone else: distant relatives, friends, and finally colleagues. But in my father's life, his friends, who were also his colleagues, had pride of place. My mother despised him for it. Whoever he ran into after a route had first pick of any gifts he'd brought back. When Ilona discovered this about him, she made sure to meet him right after his cargo was unloaded, otherwise he could've brought home only enough money to survive. Once, my father bought me a watermelon. On the way home from the garage, he bumped into an old friend. Learning that the friend had just become a father himself, my father, noting how haggard the man looked, gave him the watermelon *for his little girl*. By the time he got home, he no longer remembered that he'd been bringing back anything for me, but I knew that on the way to Astrakhan he'd stopped by an orchard, so I asked him where my watermelon was. My father just threw up his hands. My mother used to say, helpless with rage, that his buddies always came first. After his death, his friend Fyodor took on the responsibility of caring for my grandmother. He drove her to the cemetery once a month, and during harvest season he kept her in potatoes, tomatoes, and eggplant. The economics of senseless generosity had borne its modest fruit.

When everyone had said their farewells to my father, Fyodor came to me. He took me by the forearm and said quietly that I also needed to say goodbye. I went slowly toward the violet coffin atop the fresh-cut wooden sawhorse and looked into my dead father's earthen face. Sparse cold raindrops were falling on my face like light metal shavings. I had already seen his dead face in profile as we drove out to the cemetery. They'd seated me in the hearse, which was a regular van with a modified back; all the seats except those around the perimeter had been removed, and in the middle of the car the funeral home had installed a wooden beam lined with sheet metal. There was a stench in the van. A glossy black fly glided quickly along my father's leg. Ilona brushed it away, and the fly began circling and buzzing by the ceiling. When the hearse climbed onto the bridge, my grandmother wailed that Yura had crossed this bridge on his routes. And now, she moaned, he was taking his final one.

I sat listening to Ilona cry and my grandmother moan and thinking that it was strange how right up until I found myself next to my father's body I'd felt deep pangs of loss, but now that he was lying there before me, I felt nothing. I studied the texture of the dead skin, the unnatural stretch of the grayish lips. The morgue make-up artists had painted sweeping dark brows across my father's face, so that he now resembled a Tatar khan. An apricot-colored paper shirt bunched between the lapels of a cheap blazer with a metallic sheen. I suddenly saw how large my father's hands were. I'd never noticed that before. I was fully immersed in looking at this sham funeral puppetry; there was no sense of sorrow, only a sense of disappointment. It was disappointing that these things looked like disposable bric-a-brac from a newspaper kiosk. Between the white folds inside the coffin I spotted a staple, and stretching out my hand to part the fabric, I saw that the fake velvet and white satin were sloppily stapled to the wooden boards. When I touched it, the coffin felt like a sturdy crate. And I couldn't understand why Ilona and my grandmother were holding on to it as though it were my father's hand, or something living, something it made sense to hold on to. Having felt the coffin, I put my hand down on my knees, feeling the warmth of my own leg. That was being alive; when you die, you become a cold, hollow object.

Fyodor steered me through the standing crowd to my father's coffin. Now I saw his dead face from above. His sunken eyes seemed even smaller, his hair had grown out a little after a clean shave. The air smelled like fresh soil, and a light drizzle was falling on his face and shirt. Fyodor said quietly that I could kiss my father's forehead, and I held my breath as I bent down and touched my lips to the tissue-paper forehead band. With my head still bent, I glimpsed the silhouettes of Jesus Christ and the Virgin printed sloppily in black ink. And pulling back from the darkness of the last kiss, I saw the snow-white interior of the coffin lid. As soon as I lifted my head they closed the coffin and began nailing it shut. The white sky of the steppe promptly swallowed up the dull echoing blows of the hammers. Women sobbed quietly after every thud. I threw down my handful of earth and retreated. Squatting down ten meters or so from my father's grave, I adjusted my dress between my thighs and lit a cigarette. The rain kept falling, and the steppe lay wide open and plain.

The gravediggers worked quickly. The truckers' wives spread a vinyl tablecloth on a table by a neighboring grave and put out sliced pies, cucumbers and tomatoes, a few bottles of vodka. People approached the table four at a time and drank, and the women pouring out the vodka called up the next group. Come drink to his memory, they called. I, too, went and drank the vodka. They poured it into a little plastic cup for me, and I chased it with a sour pickle, a slice to which a large, softening pie crumb had stuck. Everyone got one drink, and the women poured shots for the gravediggers so they could join, too. After the first round, Fyodor started rushing us along—the mortuary staff worked by the hour, and we had to let them go, but to do that we needed to decide whether anyone was returning in the hearse.

When my mother told Fyodor that my father had died of AIDS, he didn't believe her. His proof was that he and my father had eaten from the same plates and used the same towel. My mother explained that HIV and AIDS can't be spread that way, but Fyodor still regarded the news with a great deal of suspicion. So then where, he asked my mother, would Yura have picked it up? Fyodor talked like a native Astrakhaner, singingly, drawing out his final syllables. It was particularly noticeable when he asked a question or talked about something with regret. My mother used to do impressions of Astrakhan speech, and my father would joke that at the airport you didn't need to check the flight board to find the Astrakhan plane, just follow the people clucking and cooing like a bird market. Whenever I spent a little time in Astrakhan I started speaking that way, too, but when I left, I'd lose the accent quickly; it couldn't last long layered over my choppy Siberian talk. Fyodor's question implied neither fear nor disgust; he was genuinely confused. My father's death was a great loss for him, but he wasn't particularly concerned about its cause, since it had already happened. Maybe at night, after his kids were asleep and the daytime bustle had died down, he talked it over with his wife. Maybe he was surprised, or even angry with my father. Fyodor, raised in a village and devoted to a patriarchal system and family values, may have considered my father a great friend, but Yura remained a mystery to him. For Fyodor, trucking was a way to support a large family, while for my father it was a way of life. The darkness within my father attracted people; they pitied him, and they admired his freedom.

I understood Ilona's fears. Over thirty years in Russia, HIV had become mythologized as a *shameful*, mortally dangerous disease. I had a different view, now, of their life together, their relationship. Ilona kept a few bottles of rubbing alcohol under the table and often wiped down the household surfaces and any pointed or sharp objects. I've already said that I don't know whether my father had ever gone to the regional AIDS center, but after talking to Ilona I understood that she wasn't on any medication, either. HIV, for her, meant inevitable death. Her wailing above my father's coffin was a lament of her own doom. There were already rumors going around that my father had died in great pain, but nobody knew what had caused it.

Back in the blue room, I'd tried to remember everything I knew about AIDS. I remembered the slogan "AIDS is the plague of the twenty-first century," and I remembered issues of the *SPEED-Info* tabloid stacked in our bathroom when I was a kid, *SPEED* sounding like the Russian acronym for the disease. Sitting on the toilet, I looked at pictures of half-naked celebrities and read headlines about child prostitutes, homosexuality, and the sexual proclivities of aliens. The meanings of certain words were not very clear to me, so I skipped over headlines like "Sperm Cures Cancer." But I had been interested in an article called "The Particulars of the Female Orgasm." I thought the editors had made a mistake and printed *orgasm* when they meant *organism*, though after reading the short piece on the female orgasm, I still had no idea what the article was about. The writers seemed concerned with "your partner" and "satisfaction," and the typo in *organism* occurred in every instance of the word. Still, I paged attentively through *SPEED-Info* because I thought that the magazine was named after the horrible disease I'd heard about in the courtyard. A girl friend had told me that when you went downstairs you shouldn't hold on to the railings, because people with AIDS stuck contaminated needles into them. Talk like that made me nervous; I thought everything that sounded like the word *AIDS* was contaminated somehow, and I turned the tabloid's pages with a sense of dread. Imagining needles in the railings, I wondered at the technical aspect: How could you lodge a needle in there so that the sharp end sticks out and it doesn't fall? And what motivated those people? Was it really hatred? Or was it a terrible resentment of the fact that they were doomed?

I remembered a dream I'd had in the spring. I'd written it down— it was important to record something that defied any sort of logic. In the dream I saw my father, who smiled at me and handed me two packages of ice cream. Then everything dissolved in darkness, and I found myself in the entryway of our apartment building in Siberia. Sitting on the steps, I opened one of the packages and took out a melting ice cream cone. The sodden cone crumpled as I held it, and I felt a sharp pinch—from inside the cone protruded a long, sharp needle. A cold fear spread through my body, and I cried out in my sleep that my father had been unfair to me.

Thinking about the dream made me want to smoke, and I walked quietly out of the house and along the wooden pathway to the outhouse, then squatted down between raspberry bushes and lit a cigarette. My father died of AIDS, I thought, watching the white cigarette smoke float through the indigo steppe night. Mentally, I ran through all the infographics about AIDS I'd seen in the metro. The story they told was that the only way to stay safe was to be faithful to your sexual partner. There wasn't a single word about injectable drugs. All the flyers depicted a happy heterosexual family. In the mid-aughts, my mother had had an acute case of psoriasis that sent her to the skin-and-neurological-diseases unit in the hospital, where for lack of space they'd put her in a ward with women who had HIV. At first she threw a fit, but then it was explained to her that HIV was a virus that destroyed your immune system but could only be transmitted sexually, via injection, or by a mother to her child. I visited her in the hospital, and she told me that she'd befriended *this one sweet druggie*.

I was thinking about the shame I'd felt when I heard that my father died of AIDS. I found it difficult to even say the words *my father died of AIDS*. The difficulty stemmed from the fact that my father had acquired the disease in a *dirty way*—through shooting up or sexually, the way he passed it on to Ilona. Hell, he could have spread it across the country, I thought. He was a long-distance trucker, who knows who he had sex with, or in what circumstances. Later, reading and listening to materials about HIV and AIDS, I learned that women frequently acquire the disease in the context of a long-term, monogamous relationship. Sontag wrote that in the popular imagination AIDS was a disease of outcast, feeble, morally compromised people. I read that two years after my father's death. I was feeling nauseated from smoking, but I took out another cigarette and lit it.

My father had died of AIDS, and that was painful to think about. Sontag wrote that AIDS is a disease of pariahs and members of "high-risk" groups, to which my father belonged. The thought disturbed me. Sitting in the raspberry bushes and thinking about my father's death, I didn't yet know that he'd had a high chance of survival. It was only when I returned to Moscow that I went online and discovered there was a treatment for HIV. My father found out his status during his first bout of illness. He had probably been directed to go to the regional AIDS center, but he never did, because he assumed that he was going to die. A regimen of antiretroviral drugs requires discipline and responsibility for one's health. It was impossible to expect such things from my father. Remember the guy I wanted to ask about meningitis, but couldn't, because he died? He died because he quit taking his pills several times and then wound up in the hospital with meningitis. Now I know that in Russia the AIDS services work in such a way that a patient may not be prescribed the drugs immediately; people have to wait to develop a certain viral load to qualify for a prescription. Before that, they have to go through several stages of examinations and wait to see a virus specialist. My father would never have bothered doing all that.

The cause of my father's death was a combination of AIDS myths, institutional red tape, and his own carelessness.

My phone vibrated: it was a message from Veronika, asking me about the trip. I didn't feel like answering her. I couldn't accept that anything else existed but the plot of land on which I stood. Maybe while I was on the train the steppe had swallowed up the entire world, and there was nothing left of it but this small stand-alone house with a raspberry orchard and an outdoor toilet. And somewhere else in the steppe there was a large sectioned refrigerator in which my father's body was stored. Veronika's message seemed like an illusion. I opened the text, put out my cigarette, and responded: *it's fucked, tell you when back*. I didn't want to go back. I wasn't in love with Veronika. There in the raspberry bushes by the toilet I felt that I didn't love anyone or anything at all. The blue-black night was endless and blind. It needed nothing in order to exist. I wanted to be someone who needed nothing in order to exist. I didn't want to feel ashamed, I didn't want to feel the pain and the ambivalent pity bubbling up inside me and tormenting me.

I did want to sleep, so I went back to the blue room, took off my pants, and covered myself with the polyester blanket. In the blue light, the flowers printed on the blanket cover glowed, and it smelled powerfully of Tide powder. Ilona always put in heaps of detergent powder, and in the cabin of my father's truck the smell would hold for the first three days of a route. Gradually it faded, yielding to the smells of fuel oil and diesel.

My father's death seemed accidental. Torn out of the world. But it wasn't like that at all. Rather, his dead body had drawn everything into itself. It wasn't empty, it was riddled with meaning. It was the material manifestation of the history of the overwhelming majority of his generation of Russian men. You keep thinking that things happen all by themselves, but that is not the case. Everything has its causes and its consequences. The world is a coherent thing, but even abandonment has a source. Even I had a father.

19

Sometimes a small wisp of cloud hovers above the steppe. In windless weather it can hang there for an hour without moving. I like thinking about massed water particles like this. They seem fine and fragile, like delicate tracing paper, but they inspire a kind of melancholy, because this motionless white dot above the flat earth gives rise to a sensation of total stillness.

When I was a child I often dreamed of a desert horizon cleaving the world into pale sky and yellow earth. In my dream, I saw the distance more and more clearly, and eventually, at the horizon line, I noticed a tiny post shaking in the wind that swept the far-off sand. In the dream I was trying to get to the post. I knew that if I reached the post, something important would be revealed to me. I knew that the world contained a mystery, but I wasn't trying to understand it to gain power over things. I just wanted to touch the mystery, because the encounter would bring me relief, freedom from my dark thoughts. Dreaming, I strained for the horizon, though I didn't feel myself to have a body. I was flying there, all of me becoming a single gaze directed toward the post. But as I drew closer, the law of the horizon went into effect. My destination moved farther away at the same rate as I approached it. And my flight was accompanied by an onerous, otherworldly silence. There was wind in this desert, but it was mute, and my voice, which in the dream I tried to use to slash through space, kept breaking off before I could make a sound. With a last desperate thrust forward, I would wake in a cold sweat, crying in disappointment. I hated the dream, but I kept dreaming and dreaming it. Each time I found myself inside the dream I recognized it, and though I knew how it would end, I kept on trying to reach the horizon.

The quiet steppe resembles my childhood nightmare.

I've told you that I want to become a restless tongue, feeling the world like a dark, wet mouth, finding its chips, blisters, and cracks. When I saw the steppe I wanted to capture it. But a tongue isn't enough for the steppe. Nothing is enough for the steppe. There's not a thing in the world that can cover the steppe with itself entirely. The steppe requires a song with words as precise as an instrument for seeing the most distant stars. But I had no words, and it was as though I didn't even exist. My father existed, and the steppe existed, too. But there were no words and no me.

We had stopped in the steppe to wait for a crane to come and load us with pipe. My father spread a quilt on the ground and lay down on it with his newspaper. Nothing bothered or concerned him. He was where he was supposed to be; he was waiting. He breathed loudly, mindlessly fingering the hairs on his stomach and crushing a wooden toothpick between his teeth until its end resembled a little brush. Noticing this, my father shifted the toothpick farther into his mouth and went on chewing.

I sat next to him. There was no cell service. The sky was orange, like the steppe sand. Then it shifted imperceptibly into blue-gray and faded to lilac. Any moment now dusk would settle. When we were in the café in Vladimir, my father had asked me if I remembered the steppe. I remembered white thickets of silverberry and the brownish verdure of the Volzhsky bottomlands. To this he replied that once I saw the steppe I would most definitely want to write a poem about it. After sitting next to him awhile I got up to stretch my legs. Two weeks of shaking in the truck had made me unsteady. I walked into the steppe, which felt airless and took up all existing space. The steppe astonished me, and I was afraid of it.

I walked through the steppe with the wind booming around me and riffling the fine hairs on my arms and legs. The slow wind brought the sound of bleating and the smell of manure, and I turned around—there was a flock of black sheep walking toward the truck, and behind them, astride a sturdy bay horse, a shepherd in a blue windbreaker. The shepherd approached my recumbent father and said something to him. My father stood up unhurriedly and climbed into the cabin. From his gestures I understood that my father was sharing his cigarettes. The shepherd took the cigarettes, and my father sat on the quilt and lit one. The wind now brought the smell of smoke.

The steppe swallows time, and now I was watching a few rams fold their legs gracelessly to lie down by the canvas-covered trailer of my father's truck. The men were talking to each other, a regular conversation of the sort that happens on the road. I couldn't hear what they were saying, but I could guess that they were agreeing that the midges had been out a long time this year, meaning that it would be a good year for fishing, and my father was telling the shepherd about the fires in central Russia and the impenetrable white smog we had driven through. They were discussing the price of diesel and the winter that wouldn't come for a while but would come someday, that was certain. The true content of their conversation was this: by talking about insects and smoke, each man was indicating to the other *I won't hurt you*. My father was an outsider, the shepherd was on his own land. My father had shown the shepherd that although he was just driving through, he knew the area and meant no harm. The cigarettes were something like a tribute to the man on whose trail my father had decided to set up camp.

After two or three cigarettes they said goodbye like people who had known each other their whole lives and would certainly meet again. I sat on a small steppe tussock, smoking and watching them from a distance of a few hundred meters.

From this spot I could see how tiny my father's truck really was. It stood there like a toy car in a sandbox. I stretched out my arm and caught the truck between my pointer and my thumb. That was the only entertainment the steppe offered. The steppe played with me, and its instrument was scale.

The sheep began to bleat anxiously and rose, and I heard the rumbling of an approaching KAMAZ truck. The shepherd circled on his horse, shouted a few times, and began to lead the flock away. A half-naked, big-bellied guy hopped out of the arriving red truck and shook hands with my father. My father climbed into his cabin, then the two of them settled down on the quilt. From their bustling I understood that they were boiling water for tea.

Night was coming, and it became clear to me that nobody was going to drive anywhere in the twilight. We would spend the night here, and in the morning, when the red truck disappeared beyond the horizon, we would go on waiting. In the darkening evening, the two flat-nosed trucks stood facing each other, and by their wheels two languid men sat smoking and looking out into the steppe. They carried on their quiet conversation, and I didn't exist for them—I was on my own, like the steppe grass.

— 20 —

Your father lies crushed by the weight of water
He is the volume of the wave, he's coral.

—POLINA BARSKOVA

istening to my drunken father was a disappointment.
When he told me over the phone that he was working as
a long-distance trucker I imagined a freewheeling kind
of life, but the trucking life turned out to be impoverished
and dull. I'd hoped to have a real conversation with my father, but
he hadn't said a word regarding anything I cared about, though I
myself wasn't exactly sure what that was. My father had told me
that he felt immensely guilty about not doing anything to keep
the family together. But these were empty words. He forced them
out as though an old, heavy load inside him had been pressing
them down and only vodka could lift the load and let loose this
unconvincing confession of his bewilderment and shame. But the
confession only made me feel worse. His guilt didn't bring us any
closer together; it did the opposite. It made me distant.

My father's suffering seemed perfunctory. I wasn't hurt by
my parents' divorce. Thinking about my father, I finally realized
that he was searching for the reason his life had fallen apart. It

was important for him to discover, somewhere in his past, a single decision on which he could blame all his unsettledness, as though his entire life could be divided into a *before* and *after*. But I didn't believe in his *before*. My mother had tried to leave him several times, and once even rented an apartment and moved our things there—we had just managed to put away the dishes and make the beds when there was a knock at the door. My mother opened it; my father stood at the threshold. Silently, he gathered into bags all our things and the crystal my mother had brought. My mother said nothing. She sat in an armchair, her face frozen. I could feel, in that moment, her fear and her revulsion. She was afraid of the suffocating closeness of this tiny town, where it took her husband no more than two hours to find out where she'd gone.

A few months before my father left for good, he and my mother came to see me at my grandmother Valentina's, because I'd been bitten by a dog. Graf was a mean black German shepherd, feared by everyone in the neighborhood. My grandmother went to the house where Graf lived when she needed to call my mother, since she didn't have a phone of her own. Graf's owners had grandchildren who were always teasing me, and on that fateful day I yelled something back. The boys threatened to release the dog. I thought they were bluffing, because I knew Graf could easily tear out my throat, and the boys knew it, too, so they could only be trying to scare me.

Suddenly I heard the click of the leash clip and the curt command *Graf, attack!* From the roof of a garden shed, the black dog dove like a giant fish over the fence; he landed on a stack of logs and from there jumped to a dank pile of wood chips. I was standing in the middle of the road and knew I had to make it through the open garden gate. I was at the fence when I heard the boys yelling—they'd seen that the dog had obeyed the command perfectly and was catching up to me, and they were calling out to him: *Graf, back!* Then I felt a dull pain in my left buttock. Graf had grabbed onto my rear end, and then, obeying the command, immediately let me go. I slipped through the gate, slammed it shut, and locked it with a big rusty latch and a wooden turnpiece.

The shimmery fabric of my bicycle shorts was already soaked in dark blood. I peered into the window: there was no one in the house. Dry birch smoke was rising above the little banya. It was Saturday, Grandma was steaming herself. I walked toward the banya slowly, looking up at the sky. Usually Grandma would steam till sunset, then sit on a bench by the house drinking boiled tea from a faceted glass. Unwilling to intrude on her leisure time, I stopped by the banya door, waiting for her to finish washing. Thick blood, reeking of iron, was dripping past my knee and falling on the wooden path. My left buttock ached. From the banya came the clatter of the aluminum pitcher my grandmother used to cool down the large bucket of boiling water. I pulled my shorts away from the skin to check on the bite: three holes with ragged edges. I felt sorrier about the shorts than about my butt. Nobody saw my butt, and it would heal, but everyone could see me walking around with holes in my shorts. They were ruined now. Slowly, my grandmother opened the door, balancing a basin with her freshly washed bra and voluminous cotton underwear. She turned her brown eyes on me questioningly. What are you standing here for, she asked, not particularly curious about the reason, but just to say something. She started maneuvering around me, still holding the white basin, when I quietly told her that the neighbors' dog had bitten me. Her face changed; she rushed to stow the basin beneath a burdock bush and started spinning me around and asking me what happened.

The following morning my grandmother wouldn't let me leave the yard, ordering me to help her weed the radishes instead. Squatting, I tried to differentiate between weeds and young radish greens; when I accidentally pulled out a just-sprouted bunch of radishes, I'd sneak a look at my grandmother to see if she'd noticed I was ruining her plantings, then quickly shove the pink seedling back into the earth. All of a sudden, the gate swung open, and I saw my father. He was carrying a large navy-blue bag with a picture of tree decorations, which he put down by the fence, telling my grandmother he'd brought treats. She looked back at him nervously, which made no sense to me. My grandmother liked her son-in-law and was always glad to see him, but now she was looking at him with mistrust. My mother came into the yard following my father. She was wearing a large pair of sunglasses, behind which her face was a mass of hideous green and raspberry-red bruises. It was an overcast day in June, gathering rain. When my mother tried to smile at me, I saw that one of her front teeth was broken. The skin on her lip hadn't yet healed, baring a deep red crack. She quickly explained that a week ago she and my father had been in a car accident, and she'd hit her head. I looked at my father, who stood there smiling, hands in the pockets of his wide-legged slacks. They'd been hoping to wait for the bruises to fade before coming to pick me up. But Graf the dog ruined their plans, so they made up this story about a car accident.

No way there was an accident, I thought to myself, drinking tea to wash down the dry cake with hard pink icing that my father had brought in his blue bag. The cake was too sweet, and the icing crumbled when my grandmother cut the cake into slices and served them in little crystal dishes. I knew for certain there hadn't been an accident, but I couldn't understand what had happened that required my parents to lie to me. And why was my grandmother being so cold? I wondered. My father kept going out to smoke by the side of the house, and my mother giggled artificially at everything. She and my grandmother pulled down the shorts Grandma had mended last night to make sure that the bite hadn't become infected. It hadn't, and a singed scrap of Graf's fur, which my grandmother had pressed against the bitten flesh yesterday as a ward against rabies, had absorbed any moisture seeping from the wound, so the three dark holes were already encrusted with tough, bloody scabs. That's all right, my mother said, he didn't bite you, he just took a little taste. It'll heal before you know it. My butt hurt, and I half sat on my chair, lifting the bitten half.

About a decade later, drunk, my mother told me that my father had smashed her head against the radiator until she lost consciousness. My mother talked about that night with a vague, malicious glee. She spoke through clenched teeth, and I wasn't sure whether the target of her malice was my father, who when he found out she'd cheated couldn't handle his rage and nearly murdered his wife, or me. Telling me that he had raped her on the kitchen floor in a puddle of blood, my mother knew that she was sowing me with a horrified disappointment in my father. She had hated him all these years and held on to this story just for me. I could feel it. It hurt to listen to her, but I couldn't do otherwise. I knew my father had been brutal.

Even now, I'd rather not talk about this. But not to speak of my father's mindless cruelty is to render him a mysterious continent of inscrutable sadness and playful nonchalance. For a long time, I'd thought that unlike my mother, my father was innocent. He was always away, at the garage or at work, but I thought I could depend on him. At kindergarten I could pretend to have a stomachache, and the teacher would call my father's portable phone and ask him to pick me up. Once he brought me a live turtle in a cardboard stereo box.

In the winter of 1995 I caught chickenpox and gave it to my father. When I woke up in the mornings and went into the hall, I'd see that my mother had already left for her job at the factory, while in the room that served as our living room and their bedroom, my father lay on the foldout sofa reading a newspaper. His arms and face were covered in green splotches. I'd lie down next to him and turn on the TV, and together we would watch the morning shows. Winter days in Siberia can be dull gray or blindingly blue, but one thing is invariably true: they are short. At four o'clock, the world beyond our windows went blue black. By the time my mother came home we had to make sure the apartment was tidy and the dishes were clean. My father sent me to straighten the covers on the armchairs while he rewashed the dishes I had attempted. My mother would come home and ask what we ate all day, and we'd have to make something up, for instance that we'd warmed up yesterday's leftover soup. Then she'd peer into the fridge and tell us off for eating all the eggs.

My father had told me that the dish he made was called *gogol-mogol*. He'd take two faceted glasses and crack two eggs into each, then beat the eggs forcefully with a fork, crumble some moist bread into the glasses, and sprinkle salt over the mix. The main thing, he said, is for the bread to soak up the egg, it'll taste good then. Just wait awhile, he told me, but I couldn't wait, I ate the bread and drank the gooey eggs. I liked that the brown crust had a bitter tinge. It was hard and smelled charred, like fire. One day we had three of my father's *gogol-mogol*s and did not touch the soup at all.

All our household sheets and towels were stained blue by the *ʒelyonka* antiseptic we daubed on ourselves, which I actually liked, too. I liked that the *ʒelyonka* left a mark on things. This meant my sickness was real and that I existed. In the dark evenings we lay on the sofa and waited for my mother to return. Everything came alive and filled with meaning when she was there; in her absence things were ugly and pointless. My mother came home from work and went to work again, rewashing the dishes my father had rinsed after my attempt to wash them. Then she readjusted the covers on the armchairs. While she was gone we had interfered with her order, which annoyed her. We were home sick, we were her children.

My father was a dark continent, but my mother often said, with revulsion, that I took after him. I thought of him as my brother, my ally in troubled times, my rival in the fight for my mother's attention. He was my father, and when I thought of him I felt a bitter sense of longing. He was a mysterious continent, and at the same time he was my dark side.

One night, during the winter holidays, my mother woke me up and said we were going to visit some friends. I was taken to a house, not an apartment, and seated at a table with grown-ups. Yellow lamplight illuminated the furnishings, which reminded me somehow of my grandmother Valentina's. At the center of the table stood a large serving dish piled with different kinds of candy, among which I most coveted the white wedges of Choco Pie. I'd only tried Choco Pies a few times, when other girls brought sweets for the entire class on their birthdays. For my own birthday my mother sent me to school with a sack of Masks or Burevestniks, but the Choco Pie was more interesting; I liked the dry biscuits and the sticky white marshmallow paste. I asked for Choco Pies and ate four of them. I was very sleepy, but adults flushed with drink kept wandering through the yellow room. I didn't know any of them.

I peered into the adjoining room, which was dark, with a large stereo system lighting up pink and blue as it played loud music. A few people were dancing in the lights. My mother said I could have as much candy as I wanted, so I helped myself to a few more packets of Choco Pie and two candies in unfamiliar wrappers, and then my mother brought me to a farther room, where everything was quiet. She said that tomorrow morning we'd wash at the banya and then go sledding. She peeled off my winter pants and sweater. I was worried that while I slept the sweets would disappear, so I hid them beneath my pillow. My mother stroked my head, and the golden rings on her long cool fingers clinked gently. She straightened the collar of her wool sweater and went out. The room was dark; it smelled of damp down and something sour. I didn't like sleeping in other people's houses, where I found the unfamiliar smells and objects disturbing. Touching the sweets beneath my pillow, I rolled over to face the patterned rug hanging on the wall. The rug did seem somewhat familiar, which was reassuring. I traced the cream-colored design with my finger, and a deep sleep came over me.

Through my sleep I felt cold and light. Someone was shaking me by the shoulders; I opened my eyes with effort and saw my father's angry mouth. Seeing that I was awake, he hissed that I was a disgusting little traitor and threw my clothes at me. The room was freezing. The whole house had cooled significantly in the night, and the final remnants of warmth had fled when my father left the door standing open. Rushing to dress myself, I stuffed my pockets with sweets. My mother appeared, bundled me into my fur coat and fox-fur hat, picked me up, and carried me outside. In the yard she pressed my head forcefully into her shoulder, and I smelled her shearling jacket, warm in the frost. She carried me through the yard and seated me in the back of my father's car. After shutting the door, she walked around the car and sat in the front, next to the driver's seat. The car was running but still cold inside, because my father had left the car door open, too. The scent of frost mingled with the smells of exhaust and the air freshener.

My mother said nothing. She reached for the dashboard and

spun the knob that controlled the heat. It grew a little warmer inside the car. I kept watching her: her face looked tired. She hadn't washed off her mascara from the night before, her eyelashes were clumped, and the glitter of her eyeshadow glimmered on her cheeks. Something was the matter, yet her face revealed nothing. Something bad, even terrible, was happening, but I couldn't understand what it was.

My mother sat staring ahead of her as white steam issued from her nostrils. After five minutes or so went by, she opened the glove compartment, took out a pack of cigarettes, and lit one, exhaling her smoke through the open window. I was afraid to ask her why we were waiting. It was obvious that we were waiting for my father. But what was he doing in that chilly house? Yesterday there had been a party and dancing; now my father was there. When my mother was carrying me out of the room where I'd slept, I had time to notice that last night's festive table was covered in empty bottles and plates holding the remains of roast chicken and salad. The dish of desserts stood untouched. Above the table hung an aroma of evaporated spirits and canned peas. The room was a mess; I knew that kind of mess, and seeing it made me sad. It destroyed the enchantment of the party. What could he be doing in there, I wondered, looking at the hoarfrost patterns on the glass.

Finally, though the glass, I saw my father. He was walking quickly down a path trodden between snowbanks. His gait was clumsy, as always. He got into in the driver's seat and put down some black object, fitting it between the seat and the gearshift. I looked closely and made out a heavy sawn-off shotgun with a wooden stock. That explained the commotion: he'd broken into the house in the morning, while the sated, drunk guests lay sleeping throughout the rooms. He'd brought a gun to frighten the men and women in the house. And what else had he done in there while we waited outside in the car? My father pressed the gas, and the car rolled down the country road. I looked through the window at the houses flying by, the tall banks of snow. Dogs barked in our wake. My mother finished her cigarette and tossed the stub through the window. My father reached for the tape player and pressed play; the speakers began to issue Mikhail Krug's "Rose." He furiously spun the knob to maximum volume and pressed down harder on the gas. The cherry-red '99 roared and groaned as it sped between the snowbanks. Occasionally my father's right hand brushed against the gun, and the barrel jangled quietly. My mother went on staring straight ahead. I couldn't tell what she was feeling. I couldn't tell why my father was so angry. Out of habit, I put both hands on the back of my father's seat, by his shoulders. Feeling the nearness of my body, my father jerked around and slowly, through clenched teeth, said: *you're no daughter of mine*. The air grew thick, and I felt that I had physically lost control of myself. I was still sitting there holding his seat with both hands, as I had been a second ago. Yet the muscles of my face had gone numb; I wanted to say something to him in reply but found I couldn't open my mouth. I was inside my own paralyzed body, and I could not get out of it.

Sitting in the cabin of his truck at the Rybinsk Reservoir, my father told me what had happened that morning. I heard him out, but I had no desire to respond. He was drunk and wouldn't have heard me anyway. He spoke proudly of how everyone had panicked when they saw his gun. He admitted that he'd been ready to kill my mother and her *fucker*, the man she'd snuck away in the night to visit, bringing me with her. But he decided not to kill anyone. I didn't want to waste my life on that bastard, he said. In the yard, a guard dog had run at him, and he held back from shooting the dog, too, so as not to wake the neighborhood. He tensed, and as the growling dog was about to spring, he grabbed it by the collar and hung it on the fence. When my mother was carrying me out of the house the dog was still alive, but in the uproar no one noticed it, and it suffocated. My father talked about the dog with venomous superiority, and I listened to him speaking, looking intently into his vacant, drunk eyes. It was awful to think about the dog, who'd died because of people's hatred toward one another, the betrayals of people whose smells the dog didn't even know. I listened to my father, and a bitter lump developed at the root of my tongue; it was hard for me to breathe. In my mind I could hear the whining of a chained mutt, the crackling of snow, and the squeak of a gate. I was no different from that dog.

And I was frightened by the malicious superiority with which he told me that he'd let my mother and that bastard keep their lives and about the wheezing of the dog he hung on the fence. I hadn't wanted to know that. I didn't want to know anything about the things my father had done. I felt responsible for all the evil he had wrought. All his crimes were an indelible dark stain I felt on myself. The stain sat tightly on me, like my own face, clenched in fear.

I'm speaking to you now, but really I'm still there, in my father's truck, and I don't want to talk about this at all. When I first heard my mother's account of how my father had raped her several times after beating her half to death, I wanted to hate him. But I didn't know how to hate him. I was desperately afraid of him.

I can't see his face. He's always sitting with his back to me, watching the road. The world out there looks like a boundless swarm of buzzing insects. Black forest swallowed up by taiga swamps, bleak light breaking between sparse aspens. Yellow sheets of corrugated metal, neon signs, and abandoned villages. The congested Moscow Ring Road, the Motherland statue's breast heaving above the Mamayev Kurgan, toxic white smoke rolling through central Russia. On the roadside, the filthy fur of a dead dog that had run into the road in the night.

On a bright May day, we gather sleep-grass, which is what Siberians call snowdrops. The large pale bulbs nestled in snow-white puffs first came up on the stony, sloping banks of the Angara River. The flowers were yellow, but even their meager color was cheering. As they bloomed, the center of each flower gave off a light scent of pollen. I wanted to pick as many as possible, and each new flower was better and more beautiful than the last. The snowdrops were riches that were about to vanish and had to be gathered hastily and with great zeal. The best were the flowers that hadn't yet fully bloomed, so that later, in the warmth of the house, the buds would open fully and last a long time, standing there in an old mayonnaise jar.

My father hangs above an abyss, grasping the roots of an elm with one hand and keeping himself upright with his feet braced against the cliff. With his other hand he passes me flowers, but

I'm afraid of these flowers, because they're the reason he's risking a fall. I take them quickly, one after another, and I ask my father to climb back up, there are plenty of spots along the slope where we can pick snowdrops without climbing down. But he says that beneath the stones hanging over the Angara the flowers are more beautiful, and no one will see their beauty there, they're doomed to wilt and fade. There are many things in the world people cannot see—sleep-grass in a crevice above a river, the bottom of the yellow Bakhtemir, a white shell in the steppe. In the absence of someone's gaze and care, these things don't stop being themselves. They don't stop being. I've thought for a long time about those seashells in the steppe. They've been there since the time when the steppe was a sea. The sea has gone, but the shells remain, weathered slowly by water and wind. In some other place lies a fragment of that shell from the bottom of the old Caspian Sea. In this way my father has lain in his steppe grave for seven years, feeding the steppe salt soil and the groundwater. His dead body will stay there for a long time yet. The shell sits in the steppe sand, dry and white. His dry and white skull, split in two, will lie in the steppe as the slow sea perishes and contracts.

OKSANA VASYAKINA is a Russian poet and curator. Her debut poetry collection, *Women's Prose*, was short-listed for the Andrei Bely Prize in 2016, and the original Russian-language edition of her novel *Wound* won the NOS Prize in 2021. *Wound* has been translated into fifteen languages.

ELINA ALTER is a writer and translator of Oksana Vasyakina's *Wound* and Alla Gorbunova's *It's the End of the World, My Love* and *(Th)ings and (Th)oughts*. Her work appears in *The Los Angeles Review of Books*, *BOMB*, *The Paris Review*, and elsewhere.